"Her name's Jolena?"

Kenzie put her face against the baby's, temporarily forgetting how awkward the situation with Jonah was. "What an unusual name, and so pretty."

"Elena's idea."

Startled, Kenzie's eyes shot back to Jonah. "Elena? But—"

Elena had been the name of Jonah's partner in the Boston PD and had never taken to Kenzie. Had he married his partner?

Jonah continued, "But we just call her Jolie. Elena said it's French for pretty or sweet."

Kenzie felt her throat tighten with longing as Jolie nestled against her. "She's very sweet." Her voice was a husky rasp.

Jonah was studying her, his face stoic. "So you named your girl Pippa."

"Phillipa, actually. Pippa for short."

"Your grandmother's name." His tone had darkened with a touch of bitterness. "One of the names on our list, as I recall."

Kenzie froze, swallowed again. Was it possible that he'd deliberately ignored her increasingly desperate messages eight years ago because he was so angry with her for breaking up with him?

Did he really have no idea he was Pippa's father?

Lillian Warner earned a master of arts in professional writing from the University of Massachusetts. After she retired from her federal career as an editor and webmaster, her next goal was to become a published author. She was thrilled when her book was picked up through a Love Inspired blitz! When she's not writing, Lillian is active as a performer and director in community theater on Cape Cod, where she lives with her husband and several rescue cats.

Books by Lillian Warner

Love Inspired

His Neighbor's Secret

Visit the Author Profile page at LoveInspired.com.

His Neighbor's Secret

LILLIAN WARNER

LOVE INSPIRED
INSPIRATIONAL ROMANCE

LOVE INSPIRED®
INSPIRATIONAL ROMANCE

Recycling programs for this product may not exist in your area.

ISBN-13: 978-1-335-93669-1

His Neighbor's Secret

Love Inspired
22 Adelaide St. West, 41st Floor
Toronto, Ontario M5H 4E3, Canada
www.LoveInspired.com

Printed in Lithuania

MIX
Paper | Supporting responsible forestry
FSC® C021394

I sought the Lord, and he heard me,
and delivered me from all my fears.
—*Psalm* 34:4

To my husband, Glenn, who has been with me
throughout my writing journey.

Chapter One

Squashing the urge to collapse onto her desk, Mackenzie Reid scanned the spacious room with critical eyes. It was the first classroom she'd ever set up and she wanted to get it as perfect as possible.

Kenzie had prepared each area for a different creative activity suitable for first through fifth grades. Cheerful colors bloomed on all sides. Pots of bright paint lined the shelves next to several easels in one corner. Fairy-tale puppets hung in a row near the miniature stage. Dress-up clothes spilled from a trunk. Another space boasted sturdy musical instruments surrounded by room for dancing.

Her young students would have fun while they experimented with the arts in preparation for the school's first ever performance, scheduled for October. And that was all that mattered. The headmistress knew that Kenzie hadn't taught since her student teaching days over ten years ago, when she was working on her bachelor's degree in early childhood education. She was still amazed that she'd gotten this job and wanted to do her absolute best, especially given everything that had gone wrong over the past couple of years.

She wouldn't allow herself to take a single step into the past. It was like walking into quicksand. The only way to look was forward. Now she was the creative arts teacher at the Good Shepherd Academy, a small private school in the heart of Massachusetts's beautiful Berkshire Mountains. She had a whole new life, so different from the old one she had no idea what to expect. This was an adventure. It was exciting. It was challenging.

It was exhausting. And she hadn't even started yet.

She took comfort in knowing the room had once been used for Sunday school classes. The school had started up in the old church building a few years ago when the new chapel was built, right across the parking lot.

For the past two years, faith and her little daughter, Pippa, had been the only things that made it possible for her to keep going.

Glancing at the oversize clock on the wall, she was surprised to see that it was already a quarter to one. She had to pull herself together and get to her first faculty meeting on time if she wanted to make a good first impression.

Which she desperately needed to do.

In a hurry to push the thought aside, Kenzie rose too hastily and had to grab the desk as the room spun around her. Squeezing her eyes shut, she took deep, slow breaths and waited for her brain and stomach to settle.

"You're fine," she whispered. "You're perfectly fine. There's absolutely nothing wrong with you."

That was what all the Boston doctors had said, and that was what she tried to believe, in spite of the strange array of symptoms that had assailed her after a week on Martha's Vineyard two years ago. She firmly believed it was Lyme disease but the doctors didn't agree.

Maybe out in the country it would be easier to find a doctor who would listen to her. She hoped so, anyway.

Her eyes opened. The room had stilled, although it was a bit out of focus. Kenzie raised her chin and strode toward the door to the unlit hallway. Her still-unsteady feet caught on the threshold, and boom, she was on the floor.

"Whoa! Are you all right?"

The man's voice came out of nowhere, forceful enough to echo through the empty corridor. Startled, Kenzie looked up, trying to blink the darkness away. "I'm fine. Just…the floor is slippery, and I was rushing to get to the faculty meeting."

"No rush. They never get these things started on time."

Something in his booming voice with its slight Boston accent stirred her memory. She peered harder at his face, a shadowed blur in the dark hall.

"Good to know." Kenzie struggled to get back on her feet with her modesty intact. Not so easy in a dress.

"Let me help." A firm hand took hold of her wrist.

"I'm fine. I can manage," she huffed.

The hand released her. "Yipes. Sorry."

After some more ungraceful flailing, Kenzie stumbled to her feet and sighed. "No, I'm sorry. I'm just so embarrassed. Not the introduction I was hoping for."

The man laughed, a pleasant, hearty sound. "You must be the new creative arts teacher."

Kenzie took a deep breath to tamp down the dizziness. "Yup, that's me."

"I'm right across the hall, in the old rec room. It's my second year teaching health and safety. Which is just a fancy name for phys ed." The big, warm hand took hold of Kenzie's and shook it. "I'm Mr. Raymond."

Kenzie felt her throat go dry.

It couldn't possibly be Jonah. Could it?

He kept talking, oblivious to Kenzie's silence. "Anyway, we should head on up there and grab some coffee before it's all gone."

She followed numbly as he guided her toward the stairs, where the lighting was better. When she took another quick glance up, her fears were confirmed.

Kenzie's heart clunked into her stomach.

Even though silver was starting to invade his thick, dark hair, even though the lines around his eyes and mouth were etched more deeply and his muscular physique showed the beginnings of dad bod, even after not seeing him for many years, Kenzie would have known him anywhere.

Jonah Raymond. The man she'd been in love with back in grad school, eight years ago. The man she'd been ready to marry the minute he asked. And when he didn't ask, the man she'd left behind for a job on the other side of the country.

Then discovered she was pregnant.

He was talking away in his hearty, cheerful voice, but Kenzie hadn't heard a word. It took her a moment to find her voice. When she did, it came out hoarse. "Jonah?"

He turned to look at her, surprised, then confused. "I'm sorry. Do I know you?"

Kenzie winced internally. She knew she'd changed but hadn't realized how much. Forcing a smile, she said, "It was a while ago. About eight years, in Boston?"

She watched recognition dawn in Jonah's eyes, followed by dismay. "Kenzie? What—what on earth are you doing here?"

His tone reminded Kenzie that their parting hadn't been bittersweet, just bitter. "I could ask you the same thing."

Jonah seemed frozen in place, one foot on the first step of the staircase. His lips barely moved when he spoke. "I've been here over a year. Moved here from Boston. You?"

"I just moved here a week ago. From Cambridge, actually."

"Really?" The crow's-feet deepened around his eyes. He was only a few years older than Kenzie, in his midthirties, but he looked older than that. "How'd you end up in Chapelton?"

"Because I got this job." Kenzie's heart was beating way too fast. Her brain spun like a Tilt-A-Whirl. With deliberate nonchalance, she held on to the stair rail to steady herself. As she did, she took a casual glance down at Jonah's left hand.

There was no missing that thick gold ring on his third finger.

"What happened to the big career? Last I knew, you were some kind of big shot in kids' TV." Jonah sounded indignant, as if he thought she'd come here on purpose to upset him.

"Oh, you know, things change." Skirting the subject of the disastrous end of her career in educational television, she cleared her throat. "Last I knew, you were a Boston cop. What happened to that?"

"Oh, you know, things change." Jonah echoed her words in a sardonic tone.

After a tense pause, Kenzie started up the stairs, still grasping the railing to keep herself steady. "Well, I don't want to be late, even if they don't start on time."

She heard a heavy sigh behind her, then Jonah's footsteps. At the top of the stairs she kept going straight.

"Do you know where the meeting is?" Jonah sounded cautious.

"I'll find it."

"Not that way, you won't."

Careful not to move too quickly, Kenzie turned back to look at him. The sight of his amused smile made her insides shiver, but she kept her face neutral. "Where, then?"

"This way." Jonah crooked a thumb in the opposite direction. "Meetings are usually held in the old sanctuary. I'll show you."

"Thanks." Kenzie held herself stiffly as they walked down the hall together. She sensed that he was looking at her, but kept her own eyes riveted ahead.

"You're welcome." His chilly inflection made it clear to Kenzie that he hadn't forgiven her.

She didn't blame him. But she had every reason to be even less forgiving. And he didn't seem to realize or acknowledge that.

Frustration tightened Kenzie's throat and threatened to strangle her. What a mess. This was the only job she had managed to get since her health took a downturn, her television career had crashed and burned, and her husband deserted her for another woman. The pay wasn't great, but at least her ex paid child support and alimony. Plus, life in this village was far more affordable than in the city. And since she was faculty, Pippa got free tuition to this small but reputable private school.

The health insurance would kick in soon and she could resume her quest for a diagnosis. Lyme disease was very common in the Berkshires, so local doctors might be more likely to listen to her.

Kenzie needed this job for her own and Pippa's sake. She had no choice but to make this work. No way was she going to let Jonah Raymond spoil it for her.

"Look." Kenzie stopped dead in the middle of the hall and glanced around to make sure no one would overhear. To be safe, she slipped into a nearby nook and gestured for Jonah to join her. In an urgent undertone she continued, "I'm not happy about this, and obviously you aren't either. But this is a new start for me and I need to make the best of it."

Jonah blinked. "O...kay..."

"So here's the deal." Kenzie summoned every ounce of determination and laser-focused her eyes on Jonah's. "Let's keep things at a distance, okay? I mean, let's be civil but not...not interact much unless we have to. Okay?"

A corner of his mouth quirked as if amused by her bossy tone. "Are you serious?"

A pleading note crept into her voice as she went on. "Absolutely serious. I think it'll be better for both of us, don't you?" When he didn't respond right away, Kenzie closed her eyes and added, "Please?"

When Kenzie opened her eyes again, bewilderment mixed with sympathy had softened Jonah's expression. "Yeah. Okay. I agree."

"Thanks," she whispered. Giving him a quick, grateful smile, she turned away and started toward the sanctuary again.

Jonah Raymond felt like he'd been stabbed in the heart and then crushed by a freight train crammed full of uncomfortable emotions. Running into Kenzie and finding out they were colleagues swept him into a state of unreality. Joy turned quickly into bitterness, which morphed into a bout of nostalgia. And that led to memories of being overwhelmed by hurt and despair.

He'd certainly never expected to see her at Good Shepherd Academy. After all, the last he'd known, she'd been a children's television producer in San Francisco. And he hadn't recognized her at first.

He found himself wondering how long it would have taken him to realize it was Kenzie if she hadn't said something. Her face had lost its cherubic roundness and the sparkle of her eyes had dimmed. Her once plump but muscular body seemed to have shrunk. Her curly strawberry blond bob was now a mass of copper waves that trailed well past her shoulder blades, bundled into a careless ponytail. Her vibrant teal dress, typical of the bold colors Kenzie favored, seemed to overwhelm her thin frame.

Strangest of all, she walked slowly and carefully, as if afraid she might fall again. Where was the purposeful stride that had been her trademark? Back when they were together, Jonah used to joke that "Getouttamyway" was Kenzie's middle name.

What had happened to her to cause such a dramatic change? And why on earth did she want to keep him at a distance? After all, she'd been the one to break up with him, not the other way around.

By now they'd reached the door to the sanctuary, which was propped open with a battered hymnal. The old-fashioned, high-ceilinged chapel buzzed with conversation and laughter as faculty members greeted one another after the long summer break.

Fighting to keep his voice neutral, Jonah turned to Kenzie. "Here we are."

Kenzie stood frozen a few feet from the door, her face so pale her freckles stood out, her blue eyes wide as if with fear.

From the corner of his eye, Jonah studied her in surprise. The Kenzie he remembered was larger-than-life, bold and adventurous. Nothing daunted her.

Again he asked himself how she'd gone from that daredevil girl to this pale, anxious woman.

As he watched, she drew in a deep breath, raised her chin and put on a brave smile.

That gesture punched Jonah right in the heart. He'd seen it many times all those years ago. It was part of Kenzie's preparation when she was about to do something she'd never done before, like giving a speech at a crowded conference, or going for a television interview, or that time he taught her how to ski and she went right for the steepest slope.

A faculty meeting at Good Shepherd Academy was nothing to be afraid of, but Jonah could see clearly that she was intimidated.

Chin up, she strode past him with her oddly hesitant gait and headed for the table sporting a colorful sign that declared it "The Caffeination Station." Puzzled, Jonah stood behind her and watched as she seized a cardboard cup and pumped decaf into it. It took her three tries to pry the top from a creamer.

As Jonah grabbed his own cup and filled it, he continued to observe Kenzie from the corner of his vision. Her hand was unsteady, her lips pursed, her eyes focused and determined as she tried and failed to put a lid on her coffee cup. Her expression became more stubborn and she tossed the recalcitrant lid into the trash before turning to face the room.

His cup filled to the brim with high-test black coffee, Jonah also turned. The Good Shepherd staff comprised only a dozen teachers, but they made enough noise for at least twice as many. Happy voices rang through the old chapel, bright as the sunshine that made the stained glass windows glow.

"They're a friendly bunch," he assured Kenzie.

She jumped at the sound of his voice, sloshing coffee out of her lidless cup and onto her hand. "Ouch!"

Jonah quickly grabbed a napkin and patted her hand dry. "Didn't mean to startle you."

"Sorry, that was clumsy," she murmured, setting her coffee on the table with trembling fingers.

"Are you okay?"

He could hear Kenzie's deep inhalation as she raised her head, proud and feisty. "Of course I am. I'm perfectly fine." She flashed him a bright smile that didn't mask the anxiety in her eyes. "Everything is great." And she started to move away.

Before he could say anything else, Mick D'Angelo jumped between him and Kenzie. "Hey, I'm Mick. I teach science. You must be the arts teacher?"

Kenzie smiled and took Mick's proffered hand. "Kenzie. Nice to meet you."

Mick turned to Jonah. "Hey, buddy, how's it going?"

"Hey, Mick. All good," he auto-responded.

"Yeah? How are the kids?" It wasn't just a casual question. Worry creased Mick's high forehead. "I know it's been over a year since you lost your wife, so hopefully they're coping okay now?"

Jonah couldn't help glancing at Kenzie, who registered Mick's words with surprise. "Excuse me," she muttered, then made her way to the back of the hall.

Jonah shrugged. "Jolie is great. Obviously she was way too young to have Elena's death affect her much, if at all. Frankie's up and down, though." He chewed his lower lip. "I thought we had a pretty good summer, all things considered, but recently he's gotten quiet and started having nightmares again."

Mick clapped him on the arm. "These things take time. For grown-ups as well as kids, so don't leave yourself out of the equation."

Jonah blinked away a sudden stinging in his eyes that Mick's words provoked. Elena and Frankie had shared a special bond. Their foster child had been so lost since she died. He didn't know what they'd do without his sister and her husband, who had forced Jonah to move in with them.

"So that new teacher?" Mick nodded toward the pew where Kenzie sat alone. "She's pretty cute, right? Maybe it's time for you to get back out there." He gave Jonah a wink. "Better go sit down. Enid's about to kick things off." Waggling his heavy eyebrows, Mick added, "Maybe sit next to that new teacher. She looks lonesome."

Once Mick sat in the front row and started talking to the English teacher, Jonah glanced back toward Kenzie and caught her staring at him. Right away she switched her gaze to another part of the room, embarrassed but defiant. Should he go sit next to her? Did she look lonely?

No, that wasn't Kenzie's sad face. That was her *don't come near me* expression. Jonah knew her well enough to keep his distance, so he plunked down next to Mick with a shrug.

As the headmistress called the meeting to order, Jonah couldn't stop wondering what had happened to the joyful, intrepid love of his life, the woman who'd ripped his heart out and thrown it away for a shiny job in children's television on the other side of the country. When he'd thought of her after they split up, which was way too often, he imagined her soaring high in her career, or skydiving, or belting out boisterous karaoke at a party.

Taking a quick glance at the clock on the wall at the back of the sanctuary, Jonah found himself worrying about how

Frankie was doing in day care. He hadn't done much socializing with other children over the summer, preferring to spend time with his family or wander around the farm they owned. Not surprising, considering the trauma he'd endured before Jonah and Elena had started fostering him. The little boy enjoyed exploring nature, which was fine but gave him far too much time alone.

Jonah sighed. His own proclivity for solitude had increased since his wife's death shortly after Jolie was born. He knew he wasn't setting a good example for his foster son by giving in to grief for so long.

Mick was right. He needed to get out there again. Not dating—no way was he ready for that, and certainly not with Kenzie—but he should make an effort to be more social. After all, he was closer to forty than thirty. It had been over a year since Elena died. Maybe if he pushed himself to be more social, Frankie would follow suit.

It was time for both of them to move on.

Chapter Two

Kenzie sat upright in the hard pew, seemingly attentive and focused as the headmistress welcomed the staff to a new school year. What she really wanted to do was lie down and close her eyes to shut out all the sensory input. She'd spent so much time at home over the past couple of years because of all her weird symptoms, it was going to take time to get used to being around people again. Right now the noise, the crowd, the light and, most of all, Jonah Raymond threatened to overwhelm her.

Jonah hadn't recognized her at first, which in itself was devastating. To her, the change had been gradual, but the last time Jonah had seen her she'd been at least twenty well-muscled pounds heavier, with short curly hair and boundless energy. Kenzie knew she'd aged more than the eight years that had passed since then, and her fighting spirit was threadbare at best. Despite what the Boston doctors said, she was sure her decline was due to a single tiny tick bite two years ago. But until she could find a local doctor, she had to power through.

Kenzie checked the time on her phone. Soon she'd be able to pick up Pippa from the church's day care center and go back to their motel. The one-room efficiency, a weekly rental, was within their budget as long as they didn't have to stay too long.

She suppressed a groan at the thought that she still needed to find them a place to live that was both large enough and cheap enough. And another week's rent on the efficiency was due today.

The sound of her own name interrupted her worrying. "Mrs. Reid, would you mind standing up and introducing yourself?" The school's headmistress, Dr. Enid Mullin, a regal African American who could have been anywhere from forty to seventy, was beaming at Kenzie from the podium.

Masking her dismay, Kenzie hauled herself to her feet using the back of the pew in front of her. Her brain kicked into auto-pilot and words flowed out in her old, fearless voice.

"Hi! I'm Mackenzie Reid, but you can call me Kenzie. After I got my master's in communication and arts education, I worked as a creative director in educational television. This is a pretty big change for me. I'm so excited to be kicking off your new creative arts department. My little Pippa will be entering second grade here. We're both looking forward to getting to know you all."

"Kenzie will be spearheading our school's first public performances, the first one in October," Dr. Mullin told the staff. "Kenzie, could you tell us anything about your plans for that?"

Fortunately, Kenzie had given that job requirement a lot of thought over the past few weeks. "The October performance will be a harvest pageant. Since classes are divided up by grade, I'll assign each group a different piece of the program. There'll be a lot of singing and a bit of dance and drama. And all classes will help make bits of scenery and costumes. It should be a lot of fun but also instructional."

With a beaming smile, Kenzie dropped back down onto the pew and breathed a sigh of relief.

When she'd mentioned her daughter, it had taken all her might to keep from glancing at Jonah to see his reaction. Did he even remember her desperate messages from eight years ago? Did he even know he was Pippa's father, or had he been so angry with her that he hadn't bothered to read any of her letters or emails? Part of her wanted to ask him outright, while another part wanted to let sleeping dogs lie.

Twenty minutes later the meeting ended. Before anyone could come over to introduce themselves and welcome her, Kenzie ducked out the back door and down the steps to the parking lot.

Once she reached the ground she paused for a moment to drink in the beauty of the late New England summer. In Boston it would be uncomfortably hot and sticky, but in the Berkshire Mountains of Western Massachusetts a gentle breeze kept things pleasant. She'd never seen a sky so blue or grass and trees such a vibrant green. As she made her way across the parking lot toward the church, Kenzie found herself feeling hopeful, despite the shock of Jonah appearing out of nowhere.

The church was just across the parking lot from the school it sponsored, but after her unusually strenuous day, the twenty-five or so yards felt like as many miles to Kenzie. A few years ago she would have sprinted across the lot in no time flat, but now it might as well have been one of the marathons she used to run.

She paused in the vestibule to catch her breath and take a peek into the sanctuary where she was to stage the harvest pageant and other performances. The Good Shepherd Academy was housed in the old clapboard church that had been built in the late 1800s. The new church wasn't glaringly modern or huge, just a bright, modest structure with lots of windows. Kenzie fully intended to go to services as soon as she and Pippa had found a place to live.

Smiling in spite of her difficulties, she turned right and followed the hallway to a good-sized, cheerful room. Several small children played with blocks and other toys, including her own little girl. A plump baby giggled in a bouncer, slapping at the tray.

"Hi there!" Diane, the day care lady, called to her with a wave. "Are you done with the meeting already?"

"Just finished. The other teachers should be along soon."

"Mommy!"

Her seven-year-old's boisterous bellow made Kenzie laugh out loud. The sturdy little redhead sporting a wild mass of curls flung herself into Kenzie's arms, causing her mother to gasp. "Oof!"

"I missed you!" Pippa hopped on her toes to peck at Kenzie's face. "Guess what! I made a friend!"

Kenzie kissed her girl back with an affectionate laugh. "I'm not surprised. Can I meet her?"

"It's a him!" Pippa was dragging her mother across the room to where a small boy sat on the floor, a pad of paper in his hands and crayons scattered all around him. "This is Frankie!"

The boy looked up at Kenzie shyly, then right back down again. He had huge dark eyes, floppy brown hair and a sweetly waifish face. Absolutely adorable.

"Hi, Frankie." Kenzie knelt down next to him. "I'm Kenzie."

When he looked uncomfortable, she got back to her feet with an effort. "He doesn't talk much," Pippa explained, "but he draws real good." At her mother's raised eyebrow, she amended, "I mean, he's a really good draw-er." Pippa sat down next to the boy and watched him coloring, her eyes rapt.

"Your girl is very outgoing."

Kenzie turned to find Diane standing next to her. "Don't I know it," she chuckled.

"I hope I'll be seeing you and Pippa at church," the petite brunette said.

"Me too." Kenzie frowned. "Hopefully soon. We're living in a motel until we find somewhere to live."

"The one out on Route 20, right?" Diane grimaced. "Not a very reputable spot, I'm afraid. But Pippa mentioned you were looking for a place, and I might have the perfect one."

"Really?" Kenzie's hopes flared up, but she squashed them back down. Too many recent disappointments forced her to be wary. "Where?"

"My house!" Diane beamed at her. "We have a couple of apartments downstairs. My brother and his kids live in one, but the smaller one is empty."

Kenzie sent up a silent prayer as she asked, "How small?"

"Oh, it's two bedrooms!" Diane assured her. "We renovated a big old farmhouse that's belonged to my family for ages. There's a ton of space, plus quite a few acres. Lots of room for kids to play!"

"Out in the country?" Although she loved the fresh air and beautiful scenery, nature held something of a horror for Kenzie.

Diane's deep brown eyes gleamed. "It's only about a stone's throw from the village. You could easily walk to school from there on a nice day." As if sensing Kenzie's hesitation, she added, "It's a Christmas tree farm, and we also have a big pumpkin patch and an apple orchard and lots of vegetables. Great place for kids, believe me."

Kenzie held her breath and prayed again. It sounded too good to be true, but Diane seemed honest and kind. Plus, she'd looked at about a dozen places in the past week, all of which were either unsuitable or too expensive for her modest teaching salary. "How much is the rent?"

The price Diane named clinched it. She didn't even need to look at the place.

"I'll take it."

With his head still reeling from seeing Kenzie after so many years, Jonah had to force himself to make small talk with his teaching colleagues. More than one of them asked if he was okay, which meant he wasn't entirely succeeding.

"Where are you today, Jonah?" Dr. Enid Mullin's aristocratic eyebrows lifted high with curiosity. "I've asked you the same question three times and you've given me three different answers, none of which make sense."

Embarrassed, Jonah gave his head a shake to clear it of thoughts of Kenzie. "Sorry. Just getting readjusted to being here, I guess."

"I was saying we miss seeing you and the kids at church. My husband keeps asking after you." The wise woman pierced him with her gaze. "Are you planning to join us again soon?"

"Um…" He groped for a way to explain his dilemma and came up empty. "Maybe?"

Jonah had attended the Good Shepherd Church across the parking lot dutifully all of last year, his first year of teaching. He'd felt indebted to the headmistress and her husband, the pastor of the church, for giving him a position he didn't feel qualified for, having spent the previous sixteen years serving as a police officer in Boston. But he'd earned a teaching certification while working on his master's in community education, and based on his work experience and interest in fitness, they felt he was a perfect fit for the position.

Enid kept studying him with that all-knowing expression. "Are you having some struggles with your faith? That's not surprising, given what you and your family have been through."

As usual, the headmistress had hit the issue on the head. Jonah sighed. "It's not so much about me, but I can't help wondering why God would let all that horrible stuff happen to Frankie," he admitted. "I mean, to lose his real mother when he was just a baby, then his foster mother. He adored Elena."

A line formed between Enid's eyebrows as she nodded. "I get it. He's just a helpless, innocent child. It's not easy to understand when things like that happen to someone who in no way deserves it."

Sudden anger pulsed through Jonah's veins. "Elena was

helping him deal with his issues, and he was doing so well. Now he's a mess again."

Enid nodded. "And you're left alone to clean it up."

"I thought he was starting to do better over the summer, but now he's back to having night terrors. And he's gone quiet again."

"Which explains why you look like you haven't slept," she commented dryly. "But I'm sure your sister and her husband pitch in."

The remark made Jonah feel like an ungrateful brother. "They do all they can, but I'm his parent. It's on me to be there for him as much as possible."

Enid put her hand on his arm. "Jonah, you were left alone with a tiny baby and a very troubled foster child. I think you're entitled to take advantage of all the help you can get. And Diane and Paul are right there and they adore those babies. I'm sure they don't see it as a burden."

Jonah knew she was right, but that didn't lessen his guilt about not being as good with Frankie as Elena had been. His late wife had been the definition of unconditional love and Frankie had flourished under her care. Since her death, at times the six-year-old seemed to regress four years when he was upset. Back to when Jonah and Elena, then partners in the Boston PD, answered a call about a crying child and found the toddler sobbing next to the body of his biological mother.

"Are you listening to me?" Enid asked gently.

"Yeah, sorry," Jonah mumbled.

"Don't be sorry. I just want to be sure you're getting what you need." Lips pursed, she gave his arm an encouraging squeeze. "You know I'm here to sit and talk anytime you like. And the same goes for Pastor Mullin. You know my husband's office is right across the parking lot, and we're both only a phone call away."

Jonah dredged up a smile that didn't quite make it to his eyes. "Thanks, Enid. I appreciate that."

She shook her head. "No man is an island, Jonah. Remember you're surrounded by people ready and willing to help you and pray with you. Come back to church and you'll see."

"Soon." Under the headmistress's steely gaze, Jonah couldn't lie. "Maybe."

"We'll keep on praying for you and your family. Don't be a stranger." With that, Enid gave him a final pat on the arm and moved on to talk to another teacher.

Jonah hastily slipped out the back door of the sanctuary, following the same path Kenzie had taken. He scanned the parking lot hoping to see her, but all he spotted was a battered red Volvo station wagon pulling out onto the road. Was that Kenzie at the wheel? He squinted against the late summer sunlight but couldn't see through the car window.

Heaving another sigh, Jonah trudged down the stone steps to the parking lot and headed to the Good Shepherd Church's day care center. His younger sister, Diane, ruled the roost, rejoicing in caring for other people's children while praying fervently to have one of her own.

The beauty of the brilliant cerulean sky overhead, the lush green grass of the grounds and the rich cyan of the Berkshire Mountains couldn't distract him from his thoughts. All he could see was Mackenzie Reid's once vibrant face, now so thin and faded he'd barely recognized her.

He'd heard she'd gotten married shortly after moving to San Francisco, to the guy she'd been dating before she met him. He remembered Greg Halloran as short and deeply serious, the latter being a strange quality for a man who worked in children's television. Although he'd clearly been disappointed, Greg had been very gracious about being thrown over for Jonah. He must have been thrilled to get her back, and she must have been eager to reunite. Maybe that had been the reason behind her breaking up with him and moving so far away at a moment's notice.

Feeling the old bitterness bubbling up inside him, Jonah stood still for a moment and fought it back down. He needed to be calm and upbeat when he picked up the kids. Little Jolie had a happy disposition, but Frankie was an emotional sponge. And the boy had more than enough feelings of his own. The last thing he needed was to add his father's heartaches to the mix.

Once he'd applied enough emotional Novocain, Jonah entered the church and walked down the hallway to the day care room.

"Hey, big bro!" As usual, Diane's effervescent greeting lifted his spirits. She stood in the center of the room, bouncing Jolie in her arms and blowing on her face as the baby laughed and squealed.

"Hey, lil' sis." Jonah spotted Frankie sitting on the floor, surrounded by discarded drawings and what looked like a thousand crayons. He squatted next to the boy. "Hey, buddy. Whatcha drawing?"

Frankie crouched closer to his artwork and muttered, "I'm not drawing. I'm coloring."

"I stand corrected. Whatcha coloring?"

"Stuff."

"What kinda stuff?"

His son lifted his shoulders in a shrug. "Whatever."

Jonah stifled a sigh. "Okay, Mr. Whatever. Can you pick up all these crayons and put them away neatly for Auntie Di?" When he leaned in to pat Frankie's head, the boy ducked.

"Thanks, Frankie!" Diane sang out.

Jonah stood up and moved back to his sister to take the baby. "Hoo-boy, someone's in a mood today," he whispered.

Diane released Jolie into Jonah's arms. "Unfortunately, it

seems to be aimed at you. He was actually interacting with some of the other kids today, especially—"

Jolie interrupted her with a deafening shriek. Her distress wasn't allayed by Jonah's attempts to soothe and distract her. "I think she's teething again." He bellowed to be heard over her crying, which made the baby wail even more loudly.

"Yikes—don't break her tiny eardrums with that gym teacher voice." Diane ran for the medicine cabinet and pulled out a tube of ointment. She took advantage of Jolie's wide-open mouth to dab some on her gums. Surprised, the little girl stopped howling and stuck a fat finger between her lips to explore. "How'd the faculty thing go?"

"Pretty good, although…" Jonah paused as he debated sharing the shock of seeing Kenzie Reid again. Diane had been on an overseas mission throughout their relationship, so she'd never met Kenzie. She'd only seen the aftermath, when her brother had been a thundercloud of self-pity for far longer than was justifiable.

"Although?" Diane prompted.

Deciding against telling her, he shrugged. "You know. Lots of work getting things set up the way I want. I'm pretty beat." He glanced over to see that Frankie had just finished loading crayons into the Tupperware container. "Hey, good job, buddy. You ready to go?"

Setting the container on a shelf, Frankie moped his way over to his father. "I guess."

"We're off to run a few errands. See you around suppertime." Jonah pecked his sister on the cheek and, Jolie in his arms, headed outside. When he turned to make sure Frankie was following, he shifted his daughter to one shoulder and held out a hand to the little boy.

Frankie looked at Jonah's big hand and stopped in his tracks, then stuffed both his own hands in his pockets and trudged to the car.

With a deep sigh, Jonah kept walking. There was no point in pushing Frankie to trust him the way he'd trusted Elena, but the dismissive gesture still bruised his heart.

After all the little boy had been through, how could Jonah possibly make Frankie feel safe and loved again?

Chapter Three

"Come on, baby girl. Just a few more boxes!"

Somehow Kenzie managed to inject encouragement into her voice when what she really felt like doing was collapsing on the sofa. But not spending another night in the motel was a priority, and once they had unloaded the last box she could get some rest.

"I'm not a baby!" Pippa underscored her protest with a stamp of her foot.

"You most certainly are not," Kenzie agreed, "and that's why you're going to pick up that box of toys and bring it inside."

"But I'm sooooo tired!"

Pippa's melodramatic tone made Kenzie shake her head. Only seven years old, the girl had the makings of an actress. "So am I, Pip," Kenzie said in a gentle voice. "But we're almost done. Then you can go look at the pond and the pretty trees, okay?"

Pippa's sulking turned to curiosity. "Mommy, why do they grow Christmas trees? I thought you got them from the store."

"We got ours from the store when we lived in the city," Kenzie explained. "But out in the country you get them from places like this."

"But they're trees!" Pippa protested. "I mean, real actual trees!"

Kenzie laughed. "In the city we got the kind that don't drop pine needles everywhere, because Daddy didn't like the mess. But I don't mind sweeping them up when they're so pretty and smell so good."

"They smell?" Pippa's astonished face made her mother laugh even more.

"They smell wonderful." Kenzie sighed, remembering childhood Christmases with her parents. Then it was just her mother, then Greg and Pippa. She swallowed, refusing to let the past in any further. "As soon as we're done bringing in the boxes, you should go sniff the one closest to the house. Then you'll see what I mean."

Intrigued, Pippa seized the box of toys and ran into the house.

Their new apartment took up half the ground floor of a sizable farmhouse overlooking a good-sized pond. The surrounding land boasted neat rows of dark green fir trees, which Kenzie figured were the Christmas trees Diane had mentioned. The sign at the top of the drive read Holiday Farm, and a smaller sign tacked underneath announced that apple-picking season was coming and pumpkins would be on sale October through November.

As soon as Pippa spotted the pond, she'd been wildly excited, so Kenzie knew she'd been right to take it. Plus, it was perfect: two bedrooms, a big living/dining area with a fireplace, a sweet little galley kitchen and—best of all—a wraparound porch with swings and rockers.

It amazed her that something she'd accepted sight unseen had turned out to be so perfect. The apartment was not at all what she'd expected when Diane handed her a key without mentioning a lease. The place was gleaming with polished wood floors and paneling, bright with fresh paint, and filled with simple, comfortable furniture.

Kenzie couldn't help feeling that God had a hand in this.

It was far better than anything she'd looked at, and the rent was more than manageable.

They shared the front entrance with their neighbors across the hall, the landlady's brother and his family. The hallway separating the two apartments was more like a foyer, wide and welcoming, with a carpeted staircase leading to the owners' residence on the second story.

"Is this my room?" Pippa was staring in amazement at the loft bed with a desk and bookcase cleverly built in underneath.

The room was much smaller than what Pippa had enjoyed in the homes Greg had provided. Kenzie braced herself for an argument. "I'd say it's made for you, don't you think?"

Pippa surprised her by giving a joyful whoop, running over to the bed and clambering up the ladder. "I love it! Can I have sleepovers with my new friends?"

Kenzie smiled at her girl's habitual optimism. "Of course you can, once we're settled in."

"It's going to be so cool to study here!" Pippa climbed back down to the floor and admired the desk. "I like that it's little. It'll be easier to keep neat."

"If I'd known that was all the motivation you needed, I'd've made sure you had a tiny bedroom years ago," Kenzie teased.

As she and Pippa hauled the last boxes inside, Kenzie heaved another sigh and looked around the living room. The squashy-looking brown sofa under the picture window was calling her name. The matching chairs looked almost as inviting. She imagined sitting there, looking out at the backyard with the picturesque pond and stately fir trees, a steaming mug of coffee resting on the pine coffee table.

Despite her exhaustion, she thanked God again for this beautiful place that seemed to have fallen into her lap.

And it was an excellent distraction from obsessing about having to work with Jonah Raymond. *God, please help me to forgive him for ignoring my messages.*

"Mommy, are you praying?" Pippa asked.

Kenzie opened her eyes. "How'd you know?"

"You had your God face on. Like this." Pippa closed her eyes and folded her hands. Then her big brown eyes—so like Jonah's—popped open again. "Is Daddy going to come visit?"

Trying not to grimace, Kenzie said, "Maybe. It's only a couple of hours from Boston." She examined her daughter's face, which showed more curiosity than sadness. Greg had never acted very fatherly to Pippa, probably because she wasn't his child. And since he'd remarried and his new wife was expecting their first child, Kenzie thought it unlikely that they'd ever see him again. "Do you miss him?"

Pippa seemed to think this over, then shrugged. "Not really. I just wondered."

"Well, he's busy with work and getting ready for the new baby, settling in with Camilla." She made herself say the name of her replacement as calmly as possible. Greg's new wife was certainly nice enough and seemed genuinely contrite about breaking up their home.

"But he's my daddy." Pippa's forehead wrinkled with confusion. "And his new baby isn't even borned yet."

Kenzie pulled Pippa into a hug. "Once we've gotten everything sorted and put away, we can ask him to visit. Okay?"

"Okay." Pippa pulled away, immediately focused on something else. "Can I go see the pond now?"

"Of course, sweetie. Just don't get too close to the water."

Pippa shot out the apartment door, through the hall and down the front steps, pelting as fast as she could go toward the rockbound pond. Kenzie gazed out the window to watch her intrepid little girl standing a few yards from the water, peering at something on the ground. Hopefully not a snake. Kenzie shuddered at the thought. Pippa was fearless and adored all of God's creatures, no matter how creepy.

Finally giving in to her fatigue, Kenzie sank onto the big

comfy sofa. As she kept a watchful eye on Pippa, she heard a car pull into the driveway out front and a man's voice calling something she couldn't make out.

Suddenly a small boy darted past the window and headed for the pond. His dark, floppy hair reminded Kenzie of the little boy Pippa had befriended earlier in the day care room. He stopped in his tracks when he saw Pippa, who had turned her head at the noise and started waving at him. She scrambled up the rocks and greeted the boy with her wide, gap-toothed grin, seemingly thrilled to see him.

That's my girl, Kenzie thought with a loving smile. Her daughter would grow up to be an ambassador if she wasn't an actress.

Another figure appeared outside the window and called out in a big, resonant voice. A tall man with dark hair, holding a squirming toddler in his arms. And for the second time that day, Kenzie's heart slid into her stomach.

Jonah Raymond. Again. What was he doing here? Could he possibly be the widowed brother Diane had said lived across the hall? His friend at the faculty meeting had said his wife had died recently, so it seemed all too possible.

With a reluctant groan, Kenzie pried herself from the sofa and hurried outdoors to join the little group.

"Mommy! Mommy!" Pippa was jumping up and down. "Remember Frankie from the day care? He's our neighbor and he goes to our school! And this is his daddy." She looked up at Jonah. "I don't know his name yet."

"Jonah," Frankie piped up.

Pippa's eyes were enormous. "Like the guy who got ate by the fish?"

"What?" Frankie looked alarmed.

"In the Bible. A fish eats this guy named Jonah." With a sage nod, Pippa added, "Some people say it was a whale, but whales can't eat people."

Jonah's booming laugh stopped abruptly when he turned and saw Kenzie. "Oh. Um. Hi again." He didn't sound pleased. "Uh…what are you doing here?"

"That's my mom," Pippa announced, then pointed to the baby in Jonah's arms. "And, Mommy, that's…" Furrowing her brow, she turned to Frankie. "Um, what's your sister's name again?"

Frankie scowled. "Jolena. We call her Jolie."

Pippa studied the chubby baby with adoration. "She's so cute! It must be so fun to have a little sister. I always wanted a little brother or sister."

Frankie kicked at a stone near his feet. "She's dumb."

"Franklin, be nice!" Jonah said sternly.

When Kenzie finally managed to talk, she couldn't keep the dismay out of her voice. "You're our neighbor?" A sudden memory came to her of Jonah talking about his sister, Diane, who'd been on a long-term mission in Haiti back when they were dating.

"Really?" Pippa, who'd been whispering to Frankie, turned back to Kenzie. "Mommy, Frankie's going to show me a snapping turtle that lives by the pond."

Kenzie shot an anxious glance at Jonah, who quickly reassured her. "It's fine. Frankie knows to keep his distance. Don't you, buddy?"

Frankie gave his father a wary look. Without a word he turned and led Pippa back toward the pond.

Jonah watched his son with a worried expression. "He's not my biggest fan today, but he sure took to your girl right away. I'm surprised. Frankie's pretty shy."

Kenzie had to swallow hard before she could respond. "Pippa has that effect on people. She's always so friendly and outgoing."

When she looked at Jonah he was smiling sadly. "Takes after her mother, I guess."

Jolie had stopped squirming in her father's arms and was staring at Kenzie with a wide, drooly grin. Then her chubby arms reached out as she leaned toward Kenzie, clearly begging to be held. Without a second thought Kenzie took the girl in her arms, where she proceeded to inspect Kenzie's curls with sticky fingers.

Jonah watched in surprise. "Guess you and your girl are magnets for my kids. Never seen Jolie do that with anyone else. Not that quick, anyway."

"Her name's Jolena?" Kenzie put her face against the baby's and reveled in the sweet scent, temporarily forgetting how awkward the situation was. "I've never met a Jolena before. What an unusual name, and so pretty."

"Elena's idea."

Startled, Kenzie's eyes shot back to Jonah. "Elena? But—" She stopped herself before she could go any further.

Elena had been the name of Jonah's partner in the Boston PD, and she'd never taken to Kenzie. Had he married her?

Jonah continued. "It's one of those— What do you call them? Hybrid names." At Kenzie's puzzled look, he explained, "Jonah and Elena, so she came up with Jolena. But we just call her Jolie. Elena said it's French for *pretty* or *sweet*."

Kenzie felt her throat tighten with longing as Jolie nestled against her. "She's very sweet." Her voice was a husky rasp.

Jonah was studying her, his face stoic. "So you named your girl Pippa."

"Philippa, actually. Pippa for short."

"Your grandmother's name." His tone had darkened with a touch of bitterness. "One of the names on our list, as I recall."

Kenzie froze, swallowed again. Was it possible that he'd deliberately ignored her increasingly desperate messages eight years ago because he was so angry with her for breaking up with him?

She knew he'd received the certified letter she'd sent as her final message. The letter informing him that he was going to be a father. She'd gotten the return receipt and held her breath waiting to hear back from him.

He never responded. Maybe he wanted to punish her. Or maybe he'd signed for the letter but thrown it away without reading it when he saw who it was from.

Was it possible that Jonah had no idea he was Pippa's father?

The look of shock on Kenzie's face made Jonah immediately regret his bitter words. After all, it was almost a decade ago that they'd been talking about baby names. And they hadn't even been engaged, so it was more like a game than anything to be taken seriously.

He forced brightness into his voice. "Your little girl looks so much like you."

That was an understatement. Pippa was a perfect duplicate of Kenzie, with her wild strawberry blond curls, fair skin and dusting of freckles across her nose. The only aberration was the little girl's eyes, which were a deep brown instead of vivid blue like Kenzie's. Pippa must have gotten those from her father, although Jonah could barely remember what Greg Halloran looked like.

But more telling than the physical resemblance between mother and daughter was the attitude: spunky, friendly and funny. All the things he remembered Kenzie being back when they were a couple. All the things that seemed to have disappeared from her personality over the intervening years.

At least she was smiling right now. It looked a bit threadbare, but she was trying. "You'd better take this baby before I drop her. She's a hefty little thing."

Jonah jumped to Kenzie's rescue, grabbing Jolie and hoisting her to his shoulder. When she started to wail in protest, he swooped her up into the air until she burst out with gleeful baby laughter.

A side-glance at Kenzie showed she was watching them with a genuine smile, and something else. A wistfulness. A hunger. A loss.

What had happened to that happy-go-lucky woman Jonah had adored? He tried to think of a way to ask that wouldn't be too intrusive but he came up empty.

A third car pulled into the driveway and stopped. As the door opened, a woman's voice called out, "Hey there!"

"Hey, sis!" Jonah answered with relief.

Diane trotted up to them, her dark eyes sparkling with excitement. "I see you guys have met!" She glanced back and forth from Jonah to Kenzie as if checking to see how they were getting along, then reached her arms out for Jolie. "Give me that baby this minute! Auntie Di needs a welcome-home smooch!"

Jolie squealed with joy as Diane covered her with kisses, although Jonah could see that his sister kept glancing at him and Kenzie. What was she looking for? Was she trying to set them up?

This was way too much of a coincidence.

Jonah narrowed his eyes and cocked an eyebrow at Diane until she noticed. She froze, looking guilty.

"We're all moved in," Kenzie was saying. "It's absolutely perfect. I can't thank you enough for offering it to me like that!"

"Like what?" Jonah asked.

Kenzie turned to Jonah. "When I went to pick up Pippa at day care, I mentioned that we were looking for a place to live and Diane told me she had an apartment ready to move into."

"Wow. That's truly an amazing coincidence." He tried to keep the sarcasm out of his voice but didn't entirely succeed.

Diane was grinning. "Wasn't it, though?"

Kenzie looked at them, probably puzzled by the vibe, then shrugged. "I'd better rescue Pippa from the snapping turtles and get her dinner ready." She shot Jonah a tight-lipped smile.

"It was nice to see you again." With that, she started walking tentatively toward the pond to find her daughter.

Jonah turned to Diane, preparing to grill her. "So, when did your guest suite become a rental?"

Unfazed, Diane bounced Jolie in her arms. "When I saw this adorable redheaded lady with an adorable little redheaded girl who needed a place to live."

"And she told you her name was Mackenzie and you remembered I once had a redheaded girlfriend by that name?"

"That's not what happened at all." Diane's eyes widened. "That's your Kenzie? Really? Because you know I never met her, right?"

"Right, but still, this is a bit much of a coincidence."

Diane was shaking her head. "I honestly had no idea." At his stern glare, she amended, "Okay, maybe just a little idea, but it was kind of a long shot. Pippa was in day care today. She told me they were living in that awful motel out on Route 20, so when her mother came to pick her up…"

"Do you know we're also teaching right across the hallway from each other?" Jonah demanded.

"On the same floor? Wow, that's a surprise." Her smile widened as if this was good news. "I mean, obviously I knew you were both teaching at the school, but…"

"She suggested that we avoid each other as much as possible." It came out sharper than he'd intended. "Which is going to be interesting if we're both living and teaching in close proximity."

"Oh!" Diane's smile disappeared with almost comical rapidity. "I had no idea—I mean, why would she want that?"

Trying to ignore the ache in his chest, Jonah shook his head. "I honestly don't know. It was her idea to break up and move across the country before her graduation. I'd been planning to propose to her after the ceremony, but…" His eyes started to sting. Embarrassed, he turned so Diane couldn't see his face. "I must have done something to upset her, but she never told me what it was."

"Well, you could ask," Diane suggested.

"No." The word came out more sad than resolute, but Jonah knew it was true. "You never met her, so you don't know what I'm up against here."

They watched as Kenzie and Pippa walked by them on their way to the porch steps. Pippa gave an energetic wave and smile but Kenzie barely looked at them.

"You could at least try…" Diane started again as soon as Kenzie was out of earshot.

"No. Diane, you don't get it. Trust me on this." Jonah sighed deeply as he took Jolie from his sister. "Once Mackenzie Reid makes up her mind about something, there's absolutely no changing it."

Chapter Four

Until the last few students waved goodbye as they left her classroom, Kenzie kept a big, warm smile plastered on her face. But as soon as she heard the final footsteps receding up the stairs, she finally let herself relax.

Which meant collapsing face-forward onto her desk with a groan. *Thank You, God. I could never have done this without You.*

There was no doubt in her mind that God had gotten her through her first full week of teaching. She'd made a start in assigning groups tasks for the harvest pageant, which most of the children seemed excited about. All her careful planning had paid off, although she'd had to improvise a few times with kids who'd called some projects boring or were too shy to participate in group activities.

Jonah's son, Frankie, was the most extreme case of the latter group. He hung back, standing apart from the other kids, seeming almost to disappear inside himself if Kenzie tried to coax him. Once she learned how much Frankie loved to draw and color, she let him stay in the art corner as much as he liked. In other words, every single creative arts class period for the entire week.

Just today during the first grade's period, she'd tried to convince the boy to spread his wings. "Wouldn't you like to try something different today? Maybe play the bongo drums or make a mask for the harvest pageant? Your grade is the parade of farm animals. Maybe you could make a horse mask?" But Frankie only shook his head decisively and headed for his favorite easel.

Tessa Adams, a fellow first grader—a pushy little girl with pigtails and braces—had tugged Kenzie's elbow. "Frankie is stupid. He doesn't like to do anything fun."

"Never call anyone stupid, Tessa," Kenzie had scolded. "It's mean. Frankie may not enjoy the same things you enjoy, but that's absolutely fine."

"All he ever does is draw pictures like a baby," Tessa said scornfully.

"Drawing is hard and Frankie does it very well." It was true. Frankie's pictures showed innate skill surprising in a six-year-old.

Tessa had scowled and stomped away to the puppet theater, muttering something under her breath about stupid art. That was how she'd earned herself Kenzie's first time-out and made the new teacher wonder if Frankie could be getting bullied. It didn't seem possible at such a small school, but it might explain why he drew back from group activities.

Kenzie knew she should discuss it with Jonah. As much as she might wish to avoid him, there was no getting around the fact that he was the father of an apparently troubled child.

Frankie's diffidence also made her wonder about what was behind it. He certainly seemed to have a solid home with a loving father, happy little sister and doting aunt. Losing his mother so recently had to be a factor in Frankie's behavior, but it seemed to Kenzie that something more was going on.

She remembered Elena Medeiros as a strong-willed beauty in her late twenties. In the time she and Jonah dated, Kenzie had only met his partner on a couple of occasions, but those fleeting encounters had been enough to convince Kenzie that

Elena had some very strong feelings for Jonah. He, of course, was oblivious.

Kenzie had been careful to avoid Jonah as much as possible, both at school and at the farm. It wasn't easy, given that they worked and lived right across from each other. Even harder since their kids had become fast friends. For the first week she'd managed to avoid him pretty well, but those days were numbered, for sure.

"Hey! Congratulations!"

Kenzie jumped a mile as the boisterous male voice rang through the room. Her eyes shot to the door to find Jonah standing there grinning at her. Her heart was already hammering from being startled, and that once familiar smile didn't slow it down any.

"You okay?" His face creased with worry as he looked at her. "Didn't mean to scare you. Sometimes I forget how loud I can be, especially after a day of teaching in a gym."

Kenzie managed a weak chuckle. "Yeah, just having a minor collapse. At least the week is over."

"That's why I wanted to congratulate you." Jonah came closer to the desk and looked down at her, concern still etched into his forehead. "You made it through your first week with flying colors. The kids absolutely love you."

"Really?" Her eyes stung at the unexpected news. Or was it the gentleness in Jonah's warm brown eyes, the kindness in his voice? Kenzie shoved down the emotion welling up inside her. It was not okay to react like that to a fellow teacher, especially one she'd been so much in love with years ago, whose child she'd been raising without him.

"Yeah, really." Jonah's smile was back, stirring something she'd buried deep inside her. She forced herself to look away. "They talk about Mrs. Reid all the time, how cool you are, how much fun they have in your class, how excited they are about the harvest pageant. And my Frankie is your biggest fan."

"Wow. I'm surprised to hear that." Kenzie ignored her aching joints and stood up. "He doesn't seem very interested in most of the class projects."

A line formed above Jonah's nose as he nodded. "He's a bit of a loner, but you're taking the right approach with him. He really loves to draw. You're letting him be himself and not pushing him to socialize."

Kenzie looked straight at Jonah. It was the perfect opportunity to express her concern and find out more about Frankie. "I'm not sure I should be encouraging that, but anytime I try to get him involved in a group project, he freezes up. Is there anything I should know about him?"

Jonah studied her for a moment, glanced at the clock on the wall. "I just sent him up to the office to drop off some papers for me. Dr. Mullin will undoubtedly spend some time talking to him, so we have a few minutes."

Kenzie nodded. "Pippa's in the library, looking for another pile of books to read this weekend."

Jonah pulled a chair next to Kenzie's desk and sat. "You should probably sit back down."

"Okay." Suppressing a sigh of relief, Kenzie plopped back into her chair. "I've been worried about him. I mean, I know he has a loving home." Actually, she didn't know that for sure. She just assumed it.

Jonah held up a hand. "Not always. I mean, not originally."

"But I've seen you with him," she persisted, then hesitated before adding, "I mean, I know your wife passed away, but…"

Looking perplexed, he cut her off again. "Let me start from the beginning, okay? It's a pretty convoluted story."

"Of course. I'm sorry." Kenzie propped her chin in her hand to look at Jonah. She couldn't help wondering what was behind his sorrowful expression as she tried to push down the tug of nostalgia. "I won't interrupt."

He leaned forward, folding his hands on her desk, and gave

her a wistful smile that made her wonder if he was having a similar struggle. "It's okay. You never were patient when it came to long stories."

Their eyes met and Kenzie felt her cheeks growing red. Ignoring the complex twist of emotion in her stomach, she managed to give a little shrug. "Please go on." At his puzzled reaction, she prompted, "About Frankie?"

"Oh! Of course." Jonah chuckled, shaking his head. "Brain like a sieve." He folded his arms across his broad chest and cleared his throat. "About four years ago—"

Pippa chose that moment to burst through the classroom door with an armload of books and Jonah's son trailing behind her. "Mommy, can Frankie and me camp out in the backyard this weekend?"

Jonah gave Kenzie a comical half smile that she remembered so well from their time together. Maybe he was remembering their own disastrous camping expedition, which was about the last thing Kenzie wanted to think about. Pushing the memory aside, she said, "Camping?"

Jonah reached for Frankie, who twitched away from him. "It's something we did during the summer."

Kenzie couldn't help feeling a jab of alarm. "But is it safe? I mean, there's a lot of wildlife around the farm, isn't there?"

"It's perfectly safe. I pitch the tent near the back door of the house so if it rains or someone gets scared, they can run right indoors." He pulled Frankie into a one-armed hug. "Right, buddy?"

Frankie leaned away from his father's embrace. Pippa let go of her friend's hand and bounced up and down in front of her mother. "So, can we, Mom? I've never camped out in my whole entire life and it sounds so cool! Frankie says there's like a zillion stars and bugs that light up and…" Her eyes grew huge. "And singing frogs!"

The look of alarm on Kenzie's face made Jonah burst out laughing. "Such a city girl!" he teased.

Kenzie's heart flipped over at the familiar old taunt. Although Jonah had become a police officer in Boston, he'd grown up in the New England countryside and loved to tease Kenzie about her "big city" ways. As the daughter of two college professors, she'd led a pretty sophisticated life, full of the arts and devoid of nature unless it was under a microscope.

"Um…let me think about it," she stammered, horrified at the thought of her little girl outside at night with nothing but a tent to protect her. What if a fox or coyote came along? She'd heard that there were coyotes in Massachusetts. And even bears.

"Please, Mommy? Please, please, please?" Hands clasped under her chin, Pippa hopped up and down with excitement.

"I said let me think," Kenzie repeated firmly. "Right now we need to head to the grocery store."

"Booooo-ring!" Pippa singsonged, then tacked on a quick "Sorry!" when Kenzie shot her a reproving look.

Feeling exhausted at the mere thought of doing anything at all, Kenzie slapped on a bright smile and got to her feet again. She turned to Jonah and said in a brusque, professional tone, "Thanks for the encouragement, by the way. I needed it."

"You're welcome." The weary smile he gave her tugged at her heart. "I'll see you back at the house. Maybe we can have our talk then."

On the drive home, Jonah glanced in the rearview mirror and tried to catch his son's eye. "So you like Mrs. Reid?"

"Yeah."

"You excited about doing the pageant?"

Staring straight ahead at the back of the seat in front of him, Frankie shrugged. Next to him, Jolie let out a squeak of pure happiness.

"What's your sister doing back there?" Jonah asked.

Frankie made an impatient sound. "She's not my sister."

Jonah couldn't help sighing at the return of their on-again, off-again argument. "Yes, she is, buddy. You're my son, she's my daughter, therefore she's your sister."

"You're not my father." The statement held more misery than a six-year-old should ever feel.

Careful to keep his tone gentle, Jonah said, "I am your father in every way that counts. Who do you live with? Who takes care of you? Who comes to your room and comforts you when you have nightmares?"

"That doesn't make you my father," Frankie muttered. Sometimes he sounded an awful lot like a teenager, which made Jonah dread the day he actually became one.

"If you want a fight, I'm not giving it to you, buddy. As far as I'm concerned, I'm your father." After a pause, Jonah added, "And I love you."

"No, you don't."

The little boy's voice quavered and Jonah felt his throat thicken. Sometimes Frankie could be a real chore, fretful and angry and obstinate, but all Jonah had to do was remind himself of where the boy had come from and everything he'd had to overcome just to function from day to day.

Elena had worked hard with Frankie and he'd come such a long way in the few years she'd been a part of his life. After her death last year, it wasn't surprising that the boy had regressed. Jonah was doing his best, but he didn't have his wife's tireless energy and endless patience.

He tried. He didn't always succeed, but God knew he tried.

But does God know? Jonah asked himself. He wasn't sure what he believed anymore. The questions he'd asked Dr. Mullin after last week's staff meeting came back to him. Why would God put Frankie through the horrors of his early childhood?

Why would God take Elena away after Frankie had learned to trust again?

Swallowing the lump in his throat, Jonah pulled into the drive past the Holiday Farm sign. Apple-picking days were in full swing and he and Frankie helped out on busy Saturdays. Then the pumpkin patch would open, followed closely by Christmas tree season. Maybe Kenzie and Pippa would want to pitch in. There was always plenty of work to be done around the farm, but autumn was especially busy.

With a sigh, he parked by the farmhouse, hopped out of the car and went to Frankie's door to unstrap him. When the boy started to run off, Jonah took his hand and wouldn't let it go when he struggled.

"Listen to me, Frank. Whether you believe it or not, I consider myself your father and I love you like crazy. And when you're done being mad at me, I'll still be here."

Frankie turned his face away, but Jonah could still see a fat tear roll down his cheek. "No, you won't," he whispered.

The words broke Jonah's heart. "Yes, I will. I promise. And that's final." He gave Frankie's hand a squeeze before letting go. The kid shot away like a rocket, pelting down the path to the pond before Jonah could stop him. Feeling like he had a boulder in his chest in place of his heart, he went to the other side of the car to get Jolie.

"Hey, big bro!"

Diane's greeting sounded less jolly than usual. She stepped off the porch and walked up to her brother gingerly, without the usual bounce in her step.

"You okay?" he asked.

She wrinkled her nose. "A little stomach upset. Probably something I ate, but you'd better keep the baby away from me just in case."

"Should you see a doctor?" Given his sister's excellent health, Jonah couldn't help feeling concerned.

Diane's hand rested on her stomach. "I'm much better, really. A few hours ago it was barf-o-rama, which is why I had to come home from work and leave Leah in charge of the kids. Now I'm just a bit sore."

"When's Paul getting home? Any update?" Diane's husband, a general practitioner, spent every September on an overseas mission. This year he was in Kenya.

"Not for a week or so." She nodded toward Frankie, who was looking under a rock at the edge of the pond. "How's he doing?"

"He's having a rough day. I think he's afraid I'm going to leave him or disappear or something."

Sympathy flooded Diane's eyes. "Poor little guy. It's hard for him to feel safe after all he's been through."

Jonah nodded, bouncing his daughter gently as she nestled into his shoulder. "Yeah. I promised him I wasn't going anywhere, but… I mean, I have no right to make that promise. I could get hit by a bus tomorrow or find out I'm fatally ill."

Diane winced. "I wish you wouldn't think like that. Frankie's not the only one who'd be lost without you."

"Sorry, but…" Jonah gazed off at the small figure trying to skip stones across the pond. Such an idyllic scene that didn't give a hint about the little boy's traumatic history. "Life is unpredictable. Horrible things happen out of nowhere. People disappear from your life without warning. Is it fair to promise I'll always be here?"

Diane studied her brother with worried eyes. "I think you had to say those words. That's what he needs to hear."

Jonah's heart ached for Frankie. "I thought he was doing okay for a while this summer, but now he seems to be struggling again."

Diane shook her head. "You've got to expect ups and downs, given what happened." Eyeing her brother, she added, "I'm sure you've been having them, too. It hasn't been that long since Elena's accident."

"She wouldn't have been in an accident if she hadn't taken those pills."

The sudden bitterness in Jonah's voice made Diane peer at him more closely. "And you haven't forgiven her for that," she said softly.

"How could she do that to us?" Jonah exploded. "Especially to Frankie. She knew what he'd been through. What was she thinking?"

"She wasn't." His sister put a calming hand on his arm. "Jonah, postpartum depression is not logical. When she took the pills, Elena was probably just thinking about feeling less pain. Most likely she felt overwhelmed and not up to the task of caring for two small children, which could also be why she left them alone to go for a drive."

"Why didn't she let me know how sad she was? Why didn't she get help?" He choked out one last question, this one more painful than the ones before. "How did I not see it?"

Frightened by her father's ragged tone, Jolie started to sniffle. He hugged her close and kissed her soft brown hair until she calmed down.

"You haven't forgiven her, but you also haven't forgiven yourself," Diane said softly. "God will help you if you let Him."

Careful not to upset Jolie, Jonah murmured, "I don't know if I trust God at all anymore."

"I know. But I'm praying for you, and I know you'll find your way back to Him." Diane smiled lovingly, then grimaced. "I'm still not feeling a hundred percent, so I'm going upstairs to lie down for a bit. Come on up later if you want company and help with the kiddos." She blew him a kiss and hurried back into the house.

As Jonah started down the path to the pond, he heard a car pull into the driveway behind him. Turning, he saw Kenzie's beat-up Volvo wagon pull into a parking spot under the ancient oaks. When she got out of the car, it was instantly clear to Jonah that she was worn out.

He secured his squirming daughter into the baby swing on the front porch. "Here, Jolie. Daddy'll be right back." Jolie kicked her fat little legs and babbled happily.

"Need some help?" he called out as Kenzie and Pippa pulled grocery bags out of the wayback.

"Nope, we're good." Somehow Kenzie's overly bright smile didn't convince Jonah.

Pippa ran up to Jonah and handed him one of the bags she was holding. "Yes, please, Mr. Raymond. We would very much like your help, thank you."

Despite his mood, Jonah couldn't help chuckling. "Well, Miss Philippa, you are very welcome. I'm most happy to help," he responded.

"Hey, how'd you know my name was Philippa?" the little girl demanded.

Jonah glanced toward Kenzie. She slammed the rear door of the wagon shut, her arms draped with several bags of groceries. "Your mom told me."

Pippa spotted Frankie down at the pond, shoved her other bag into Jonah's arms and raced down the path toward the pond. "Hey, Frankie! I'm home!" Her bellow echoed throughout the property.

Noticing how wobbly Kenzie seemed, Jonah hurried over to take some of the bags from her. "Your daughter said my help is very much appreciated."

"She's right," Kenzie admitted as they walked up the porch steps.

"Are you all right? You seem kind of unsteady."

Kenzie had frozen on the top step, blinking rapidly. She grabbed the railing, the color draining from her cheeks. "I'm just tired."

Alarmed, Jonah set the groceries on the porch and leaned in

closer to study Kenzie. "You are way more than tired, Kenz. What's going on?"

She took a breath and swallowed, squeezing her eyes shut. "No big deal. It's just a headache," she admitted. "It came on very suddenly while we were shopping. Those fluorescent lights…" She winced and swallowed again. "Sometimes they bother me."

Without waiting for her permission, Jonah helped Kenzie into the house, relieved to find the door to her apartment unlocked. He guided her inside and made her lie down on the sofa. Then he pulled down the shades.

"Do you have anything you can take? Tylenol? Aspirin?" As he asked, he remembered Kenzie's extreme sensitivity to any kind of medication, her insistence that "walking it off" was her preferred choice of dealing with pain after a marathon because even over-the-counter stuff made her dizzy and sick.

One arm over her eyes, Kenzie whispered, "I'll be okay soon. I just need to be still for a bit." With a wavering smile, she added, "Thank you."

As quickly and quietly as possible, Jonah brought in the rest of the groceries and put them away in the little kitchen. Back in the living room he asked softly, "Is there anything else I can do?"

He could barely hear Kenzie's response. "It's getting better. I guess I just needed to rest a minute." The words sounded forced as she pushed herself upright.

"You should keep resting. I'll be out on the back porch if you need me. And I'll watch out for the kids, so don't worry about Pippa."

"No, no," she insisted. "I can see them from the window. It's fine."

"Well, I need to get out there 'cause Jolie's in the bouncer."

"I'll come with you."

Jonah sighed to himself as he watched Kenzie rise. Too

many obstinate people today, first his son, now his…whatever Kenzie was. Neighbor. Fellow teacher. Ex-girlfriend.

Love of his life, until she'd yanked the rug out from under him for no apparent reason.

His protective feelings vanished as the old bitterness returned. He studied Kenzie with critical eyes. She stood stock-still for a moment as if finding her balance, then gave him a tremulous smile. "See? Much better."

"If you say so."

He strode to the door, leaving Kenzie behind. Despite the surge of anger, he found himself wondering for the millionth time what had happened to her. If you weren't used to it, a week of teaching could be exhausting. But it shouldn't affect anyone that severely.

What was she hiding?

After he grabbed Jolie from the bouncer, he headed to the back of the house to keep an eye on the other kids. When Frankie wasn't talking about Mrs. Reid, he was talking about Pippa. Jonah was grateful that the little girl had befriended his son and seemed so happy to spend time with him.

If only she wasn't Kenzie's daughter.

It was embarrassing how much it galled him to think of Kenzie having a child with someone else. On one of the sleepless nights years ago he'd googled her and discovered she'd married Greg Halloran suspiciously soon after moving to San Francisco. If Pippa was seven, that meant she'd been born within a year of their wedding. Probably less.

Maybe that was why they got married so fast.

"I'm going to sit on the swing."

Kenzie's breathy declaration roused Jonah from his reverie. The back porch offered a selection of wooden rocking chairs and a couple of old-fashioned porch swings. Kenzie dropped onto the nearest swing and leaned back with a sigh. "What an incredible view!"

Lowering Jolie to the porch so she could stomp her little feet, Jonah glanced out at the rows of green-hued firs that he'd need to prune this weekend to make sure they kept their Christmas tree shape. The rich blue pond reflected the clear sky, and the first touch of autumn colored the leaves on the trees swooping up into the towering mountains. "I never get tired of looking at that," he murmured.

"I've never seen anything so beautiful in my life."

Kenzie's comment surprised him, but he refrained from calling her "city girl" again. It was too evocative of their time as a couple. Guiding Jolie's stumbling feet over to a rocking chair, Jonah sat. After a moment's thought he asked, "So whatever happened to your big TV career?"

He heard her take in a surprised breath. Not surprising, considering his resentful tone.

But he forced himself to stay focused on Jolie, whose hands clutched his index fingers as she rocked back and forth.

Eventually Kenzie said, "You know I married Greg Halloran, right?"

Jonah had to tamp down another surge of bitterness. "Yeah, I heard."

She seemed to be thinking about what to say next. "We worked together in San Francisco. Then he got an offer from a Boston production company, so we moved back here. I…I was having some health issues, so I ended up not working for a while. Then Greg met Camilla and that was that."

Still focused on his daughter, Jonah suppressed a feeling of guilty triumph. "So that's why you're divorced."

Kenzie closed her eyes and sank deeper onto the swing. "I thought we were going to talk about Frankie." When he gave her a blank look, she added, "You know, continue the conversation we started at school?"

"Oh! Of course." Jonah shook his head. "Like I said, brain like a sieve."

"Understandable, given that you're raising two little kids on your own."

Taken aback by her directness, Jonah stammered, "Well, yeah, but I have my sister."

"You said your wife's name was Elena. Your partner when you were a cop, right?"

He pulled Jolie onto his lap and turned his eyes to Kenzie. "Yes, that's right. We got married four years back, and she died last year."

Kenzie held his gaze. "What happened? Was she sick?"

He shook his head. "She had a pretty rough pregnancy with this one. Lots of complications."

Kenzie's blue eyes brimmed with sympathy. "And that's what she died from? The complications?"

Pulling Jolie into a hug, he kissed the top of her head. "Yes, more or less."

"That's so…" The sound of children's voices drawing nearer interrupted Kenzie. "Uh-oh, here comes trouble!" she laughed.

"Mommy! Mommy! When is supper?" Pippa charged up the porch steps and pretended to faint on one of the rockers. "I'm starving to death!"

The swing bounced as Kenzie got to her feet. "Then I think we'd better have supper right away, don't you?"

"Yes!" Pippa jumped up. "Bye, Frankie!" she bellowed as she crashed through the door.

"Whoa!" Diane's voice came from just inside the door. "Guess someone's in a rush."

Kenzie called out, "Pippa, come here and say sorry to Miss Diane!"

"Sorry, Miss Diane!" Pippa yelled. "I'm starving!"

Frankie sat quietly next to Jonah and started playing with his little sister, much to Jonah's surprise. Diane stepped out onto the porch.

"Feeling better?" he asked.

"Yes, thank goodness." She leaned against the door frame. "But Kenzie doesn't look too good."

Jonah glanced at Frankie. "Hey, buddy, how about you take Jolie over to the other swing?"

"So you and Auntie Di can talk?" But Frankie's question didn't sound sarcastic. He even smiled at his father as he led Jolie to the other end of the porch.

Once they were settled on the swing, Jonah nodded at his sister. "Yeah, she said she had a headache."

"Ugh. Poor thing." Diane traced a line on the porch with the toe of her shoe. "I thought she was an athlete." When Jonah didn't respond, she added, "Didn't you guys meet doing charity runs or something like that?"

"Yes, that's right." Jonah shook his head, baffled once again by the huge change in Kenzie. "We met at a 10K to raise money for the Red Cross. She shot past me at the finish line, then turned to apologize." He smiled at the memory, temporarily forgetting his anger. "That did it."

Diane's face was puzzled. "Now I don't know if she could walk a mile without collapsing."

"She was in incredible shape when we were together, had always been an athlete, the epitome of health." He watched his kids swinging gently on the other side of the porch. "I can't imagine what happened to make such a drastic change."

"It's sad, for sure." Diane sat down next to him. "I don't think I ever really understood why you guys broke up."

"Same here." Jonah's response was sharp. "She ended things with me out of nowhere. And I'd just gone to see Mom and get Grandma's engagement ring."

Diane took a sharp breath. "Whoa! I had no idea you were going to propose."

"Honestly, I'd been ready to marry her about a month after we met." His heart ached at the memory of how much he'd adored Kenzie, how crushed he'd been when she'd broken up with him. "I don't know what happened. When I left to go see Mom I thought we both felt the same way. But when I came back, she'd accepted this incredible job offer in San Francisco and was moving there right away, with or without me."

Diane's eyebrows drew together in puzzlement. "So she asked you to move there with her?"

Jonah nodded. "And when I said I couldn't move that far away from my family, she told me we were through." Hurt and anger surged through his veins as he relived the scene. "I mean, she'd told me about the offer over the phone a couple of days before but didn't tell me she was going to take it. When I got back it was a done deal. She was packing up all her stuff and would barely look at me."

Frowning, Diane said, "That's strange."

"Maybe not so strange." Jonah scowled. "Turns out her ex worked at the station that hired her. They got married a few months after she moved. So I'm pretty sure Greg Halloran had a lot to do with her sudden change of heart."

Chapter Five

Kenzie was impressed by Holiday Farm's brisk apple-picking business. Diane and Jonah were tied up after school and on Saturdays. Frankie and Pippa pitched in. Pumpkins would go on sale in early October and the Christmas trees in November, so they all helped to keep the farm in good shape so they'd be ready in time.

Kenzie started to feel stronger as she got used to the routine and learned to pace herself. To her relief, she was having a great time teaching, especially working on preparation for the harvest pageant.

The fourth and fifth graders, comprising twelve children, including the very first class when the school was founded just a few years ago, were busy creating costumes and memorizing verses for their appearance as farmers and their families. The second and third graders—eighteen of them, including Pippa—were learning songs about farming and hymns of gratitude, while the nineteen first graders, including Frankie, made farm animal masks and learned a simple dance for the procession down the aisle.

Kenzie had the most difficulty teaching the dance—not only because she had two left feet, but because the movement made her dizzy. Jonah walked in one day while she was trying to teach the kids. He was alarmed to see her grab her desk, pale and breathless, after a few steps.

"Hey, can the gym teacher help out?" Jonah's voice was casual and friendly, but his face expressed concern.

Kenzie automatically started to tell him she was fine, but the expression on his face blunted her refusal. Then a memory of dancing with Jonah on one of their early dates wafted into her head. He was a much better dancer than she'd ever been, and it made sense for the phys ed teacher to help.

"Actually, that would be great," she admitted.

A smile briefly lit his face, but he quickly turned business-like. "Delighted to help."

Jonah caught on to the steps right away and made the dance into a sort of game. Soon the entire class was moving together as if they'd been dancing all their lives. When the dismissal bell rang and the kids ran off to their next class, Jonah gave Kenzie a terse smile. "I'd be happy to collaborate with you on the pageant, especially the physical aspect. I mean dancing, but also set stuff if you need anything built."

As much as she wanted to avoid spending more time with Jonah, Kenzie knew it would be best to have another teacher involved. Jonah was right across the hall, and given his subject area, he was the obvious choice. So instead of turning him down, she forced herself to say, "That'd be great. I'm sure the kids would love having your help."

He nodded. "Thanks. It'll be fun." For a moment he hesitated as if he wanted to say something else, but finally he just sketched a wave and left.

Kenzie sighed and sank into her chair. She thought she'd gotten used to seeing Jonah every day. Well, kind of. She'd tried to steer clear of him because she wasn't prepared to deal with the jumble of feelings he awoke in her. Although she fed her long-held anger by reminding herself of what had happened all those years ago, his moments of kindness threatened to undo her resolve. It was easier to stay aloof than to endanger herself emotionally.

She was a coward.

No, she was protecting herself. Jonah had never even acknowledged her desperate emails eight years ago, including the certified letter he'd signed for. She was right to be cautious. It seemed as if he were completely oblivious to the effect of his actions—or lack thereof—or he had forgotten all about it.

Whenever she felt herself responding to Jonah's warm brown eyes or kind smile, she reminded herself of the turmoil she'd gone through after finding she was pregnant. She was grateful not to have gone through it alone, thanks to Greg Halloran coming to her rescue and marrying her. Although in retrospect that marriage probably hadn't been the best decision.

One brilliant September afternoon, Kenzie lazed on one of the back porch swings watching Pippa and Frankie pretend they were horses galloping around the yard. When she heard someone come out of the door behind her, she prayed for it to be Diane.

"Hey there," Jonah said. "Getting some rest?"

Kenzie slipped to her feet. "I was just about to go in and start getting dinner ready."

As she made her way past Jonah and Jolie, he took her arm gently with his free hand. "Wait a minute, okay?"

She tried to pull away. "But it's already getting late."

"Why do you always take off when I show up?"

Something in his tone made her hesitate before saying, "I have some things to do, so just a few minutes, okay?"

Jonah studied her face, then shook his head and shrugged. "Okay. I just came out to see if you and Pippa want to join us for a bonfire tonight." When she started to object, he cut her off. "It's Friday, so you'll have a couple of days to get things done before school starts up again."

Pippa and Frankie had come barreling up the porch steps in time to overhear Jonah's invitation. "What's a bonfire?" Pippa demanded.

Frankie pointed toward a spot in the backyard where a few thick logs and stones circled a charred-looking mass. "It's a big fire we make over there. We cook hot dogs and marshmallows and make s'mores. We had lots of them last summer."

Pippa's eyes grew saucer-big and she turned to her mother. "Mommy? Can we? Can we *please*? We never got to sleep out because you were scared about animals."

Kenzie frowned but had to admit Pippa was right. She'd been too worried about wildlife predators to let her daughter sleep outdoors, no matter how safe Jonah and Diane insisted it was. With a sigh, she capitulated. "Okay, but you're not staying up any later than eight o'clock."

Pippa opened her mouth to protest, but at Kenzie's stern expression she snapped it shut and put on her best butter-wouldn't-melt look. "Okay, Mommy."

Then she and Frankie took off, racing each other around the house.

When Kenzie turned, she found Jonah studying her with admiration. "You need to teach me how you do that."

"Do what?"

"Get my kid to behave just by looking that way."

Kenzie couldn't suppress a chuckle. "Sorry, it's an innate talent that can't be taught. You either have it or you don't."

Jolie wrestled out of her father's arms as he set her on the porch. After teetering on unsteady feet for a few seconds, she dropped to her padded bottom and burst out laughing and clapping.

Jonah gazed down at his daughter with wistful fondness. "Elena had that talent, for sure."

As he bent over to take Jolie's hands, Kenzie said softly, "You must miss her a lot."

"I do." Jonah sighed. "We were good friends for years before we got married. I mean, we were partners in the police department, and we..." After a moment of apparent consideration, he went on. "We started spending more and more time together. Elena…she stood by me through…a lot." He shot a meaningful glance at Kenzie. "She saw me at my worst and was always there for me."

Knowing Jonah was referring to their breakup, Kenzie swallowed hard and tried to sound like his words didn't cut deep. "No wonder you fell in love with her."

Jolie threw her pudgy arms around her daddy's neck. For a moment his face was hidden behind the baby. Then he looked up at Kenzie with sorrowful eyes.

"Yes. That kind of devotion is rare, and Elena had it in spades." He choked a little as he finished speaking. Without another word, he hefted his daughter up into his arms and went back into the house.

Kenzie stared after him, squashing down a wave of sympathy. After all, this was the man who'd ignored her pleas to get in touch with her. In her emails and letters she admitted she'd made a mistake in breaking up with him. She'd told him she wanted to come back and be with him.

And he'd either ignored all those messages or chosen not to respond.

With a sigh, Kenzie recalled her first and only camping trip. Jonah had proposed the trip as a mental break before her final week of grad school, but she'd hated every minute of the chilly, lumpy, buggy discomfort.

When her tent collapsed during a sudden rainstorm, she'd taken shelter in Jonah's tent.

"Mommy!" Pippa was stomping up the porch steps, panting. "Mommy! Guess what?"

Kenzie instantly switched into mom gear, smiling at her daughter's excited tone. "What is it, Pips?"

Frankie trailed Pippa up the steps and threw himself on one of the wicker chairs. "She didn't even know what s'mores are," he said with six-year-old scorn.

"But now I do! Frankie told me! Mommy, they're made out of graham crackers and chocolate and marshmallows!"

"*Toasted* marshmallows," Frankie corrected. "You put a marshmallow on a stick and hold it over the fire till it gets melty. Then you smoosh it all together."

"And we're having them tonight!" Hands clasped, a big grin showing off her missing front teeth, Pippa bounced up and down. "Mommy, doesn't that sound amazing?"

Kenzie's heart sang at her little girl's overwhelming happiness. Pulling Pippa into a sudden hug, she said, "It sure does, sweetie. I can't wait." She gave the girl a smacking kiss on the cheek that induced giggles. "And guess what?"

"What?"

"You can stay up as late as you like!"

Pippa gasped and stared at her mother as if not believing what she'd just heard. Then she flung her arms around Kenzie's neck and peppered her with kisses. "Mommy! Thank you! I love you so much!"

Kenzie hid her big smile in Pippa's curls. Seeing her little girl so happy eased her discomfort about spending the evening in Jonah's presence.

Watching him interact with his unacknowledged daughter—especially in such a warm family setting—made Kenzie's heart ache.

In the cool dark of Jolie's nursery, Jonah tenderly laid his daughter in her crib and waited for her to stop fidgeting. Soon her soft breathing evened out and he knew she'd be sleeping for at least the next forty-five minutes. Frankie was still out playing with Pippa, and Kenzie was keeping watch, so he finally had a little time to himself.

Which meant he had time to think about Kenzie. Like he wasn't already doing that when he lay awake at night, all too aware of her presence on the other side of the hall. Like he didn't have to stop himself from dropping by her apartment or her classroom a dozen times a day.

Why did she try so hard to avoid being alone with him? She'd been the one to end their relationship.

What had he done to make her so angry? The previous weekend they'd gone on that camping trip. Neither of them had resisted temptation. But was she putting all the blame on him?

A brisk knock on the door yanked Jonah out of his reverie. His heart leaped at the thought that it might be Kenzie until his sister's voice called out. "We should probably get that fire started, don't you think? It's nearly dinnertime and the kids'll want to roast weenies!"

Jonah pushed himself out of his chair with leaden arms. Given what he'd just been thinking about, it wasn't a great idea to spend the evening with Kenzie, but Diane was right. The kids would be hungry and excited to get things going.

"I'll get Jolie up and be right there," he called back in the most cheerful voice he could muster.

An hour later the bonfire was roaring, tossing sparks into the twilight of the warm September evening. Stars began appearing one by one in the deepening blue sky, tiny diamonds on indigo velvet. It was all ridiculously romantic. Jonah took a deep breath and tried not to look at Kenzie, who was sitting on the other side of Pippa and Frankie, next to his sister.

Kenzie had pulled her wild copper curls into a high ponytail, which made her look younger. In fact, despite the new thinness of her face, by the firelight she looked much more like the energetic grad student he'd fallen for the second they met.

The kids had gobbled down fire-roasted hot dogs and melty s'mores in record time. He hadn't spent more than a few minutes with Pippa before and was pleased that Frankie's new friend was charming, funny and affectionate.

In other words, just what his son needed.

Suddenly Jonah realized that Pippa was standing right in

front of him, hands on her hips and a puzzled look on her chocolate-smeared face. "Mr. Raymond?"

He smiled at her. "Miss Halloran?"

Pippa looked surprised, then burst out laughing. "No, silly! You call me Pippa." Her big brown eyes slid toward Kenzie with a mischievous giggle. "Or Philippa Joy, if you're mad at me."

"How could anyone ever be mad at you?" Jonah asked in a mock-horrified voice.

She smiled, showing her dimples and missing front teeth. "Mommy gets mad if I'm naughty. Sometimes she calls me by all three names, which means I'm going to be sent to my room. But that hardly ever happens," Pippa hastened to add. "Anyhow, I wanted to ask you something."

"Sure! Go ahead and ask."

The little girl glanced at Frankie, who stared back at her wide-eyed. The children had some sort of silent communication. Then Pippa nodded and looked boldly at Jonah. "Are you going to get Frankie a new mommy?"

"Pippa!" Kenzie gasped. Next to her, Diane stifled a laugh.

Perplexed, Jonah took his time to answer. "Well, Pippa, that's…"

Kenzie came to his rescue. "That's not something you ask someone."

"Why not? How else am I s'posed to find out?" Pippa asked, folding her arms across her chest.

"It's a very personal question," Kenzie responded. "Getting Frankie a new mommy means that Mr. Raymond would have to get married."

Forehead creased with consternation, Pippa persisted. "But that would be nice, wouldn't it?"

All three adults fell silent, unsure of how to answer Pippa's questions. Fortunately, Frankie chose that moment to speak up.

"Daddy, can Pippa and me go looking for fireflies?"

Jonah tried to hide his surprise and pleasure at being called

Daddy. That hadn't happened for a couple of months, not since Jolie's first birthday.

He cleared his throat and gave Frankie a loving smile, careful to keep his big voice gentle. "It might be too late in the year for fireflies, but you might find something just as good."

"Singing frogs?" Pippa squealed, jumping up and down.

"It's too late for peepers, too," Jonah laughed. "But you might see possums or raccoons."

Kenzie had snapped into alert-mom mode. "Don't go too far, and stay away from the edge of the pond, okay?"

Jonah took one look at her worried face and stood. "I'll go along and keep an eye on them. Just to be sure they don't find a skunk." He gave Kenzie a reassuring smile and trailed after the kids, who were already out of earshot.

It was hard to keep his imagination from wandering to a brighter future, full of hope. Maybe Frankie was starting to heal again, now that they'd gotten past the first anniversary of Elena's death. Maybe he'd just needed a little time to realize that Jonah still loved him as if he were his own son. Maybe even though Elena was gone, everything would be okay after all.

And maybe Kenzie would come around and realize he wasn't the enemy. Maybe, in spite of their history, they could be friends.

"Daddy! Why'd you stop?"

Frankie's question snapped Jonah out of his reverie and made him realize he'd stopped in his tracks. He rubbed at his eyes, which suddenly stung, and cleared his throat.

"I'm coming, son!"

Chapter Six

Next to the crackling embers of the bonfire, Kenzie was trying not to worry about the two children roaming around the dark farm. Her heart warmed with gratitude that Jonah had gone with them. As much as he used to kid her about being a city girl, he understood that her worries were real and made sure she didn't get too anxious.

It made her wonder again if he'd actually read the messages she'd sent eight years ago, pleading with him to talk to her and finally telling him she was pregnant. The idea of Jonah heartlessly ignoring her news didn't jibe with how gentle he was with her and Pippa. The conversation he'd had with their daughter a few moments earlier had stirred up mixed feelings in Kenzie.

"What a sorry bunch of singletons we are." Sitting on the log next to Kenzie, Diane sighed and glanced at little Jolie nodding off in her well-padded carrier. "I know it's whiny, given what you and my brother have been through, but I miss Paul so much. He really loves bonfires and he's so great with Jonah's kids. He will absolutely adore your little girl."

"I thought he was supposed to be home this week," Kenzie said. After hearing Frankie rave about his fun-loving uncle, she was eager to meet Diane's husband.

"His flights got messed up. It happens." Diane's face brightened. "But he should be here in a week or so if the latest plans work out."

"I hope it does. I think it's incredibly generous of you to let him go on a mission every year."

Diane was shaking her head. "I doubt I could stop him. And God knows they need his expertise. But sometimes I'm a bit worried about where they send him."

The fear in Diane's voice gave Kenzie a pang. "I'm sure you are. I'll pray extra hard for his safety."

Diane squeezed Kenzie's hand. "Would you? Thank you so much!"

Kenzie squeezed back. "Of course I will. Since I moved here, I find myself praying more and more. I'm not sure why." After a moment of thought, she shyly added, "I only rediscovered my faith a couple of years ago, during a really difficult time in Boston. I think I feel even closer to God here."

Smiling, Diane nodded. "It's so easy to see the beauty of His creation here, isn't it?"

"Honestly, I don't see how people can miss it," Kenzie agreed.

"You know something?" Diane put her head on Kenzie's shoulder. "I knew you were a sister the minute I saw you. I don't know why, but I feel like God had a hand in your coming to live here."

"I feel the same way!" Kenzie hadn't realized how much she missed having a close friend. She couldn't imagine a better one than Diane, even if she was Jonah's sister. "I'd been praying so hard for a good place to live."

"And here you are!" Diane gave Kenzie an impetuous hug. They both stared into the fire for a minute. Then Diane peered around through the dark as if to make sure they were alone. Her voice dropped to a whisper. "Can I tell you something I haven't told a single soul yet?"

"Sure! Do I need to swear myself to secrecy?"

Diane nudged her playfully. "I trust you. Maybe because…"

She bit her lip. "Well, Pippa said something to me that made me think you'll understand."

Kenzie suppressed a jolt of alarm. "What did Pippa say?"

"Just that…well, she thought she was going to get a little brother or sister a while ago, but they never came."

Swallowing, Kenzie closed her eyes. "Greg and I tried for kids, but I couldn't seem to carry for more than a month or so."

"I'm so sorry." She felt Diane's arm slip around her shoulders. "But you have Pippa."

Kenzie fought the urge to tell her friend that Greg wasn't Pippa's father, and that Diane was actually her daughter's aunt. But if Jonah didn't want his sister to know, Kenzie wasn't going to tell her. She forced her mind back to the moment at hand.

"Yes. Of course. But we wanted more. Like three or four." Kenzie smiled wanly. "Greg was an only child and hated it. So we kept trying, but…well, none of them survived past the first month." Her throat tightened at the memory of those three little lives. She'd loved every one of them and grieved them so intensely it had affected her health.

Or so the doctors believed, refusing to acknowledge the possibility that it might have been the other way around. Kenzie was convinced that her mysterious illness had caused her to miscarry.

"Paul and I have tried, too. For years. And when we finally succeeded…" Diane's voice broke. "Well, like yours, they didn't stay around long." A huge smile lit up her face. "But now…"

The way Diane glowed had nothing to do with the firelight and told her secret better than words. "You're pregnant!" Kenzie whispered, excited for her friend.

Diane nodded. "I've made it through the first trimester for the first time, and the doctor says everything looks great. I haven't even told Paul because I didn't want to get his hopes up and have him worry about being away if something goes wrong. But the minute he gets home I'm yelling it from the rooftops."

Kenzie threw her arms around Diane. "I'm so happy for you!"

But she found her happiness for Diane tempered with something else, something bitter and sad. This was Jonah's sister, her own little girl's aunt, pregnant with Pippa's first cousin. And as much as she felt her new friend deserved this blessing, as sincerely as she meant her congratulations, Kenzie felt a familiar wave of sorrow deep inside.

The sound of approaching voices made the two women sit up and try to appear normal. Diane giggled a little as she put a finger to her lips.

Pippa staggered over to her mother and collapsed onto her lap with an enormous yawn. "How late is it, Mommy?" she asked sleepily.

"Pretty late. Way past your usual bedtime." Kenzie pulled her daughter close and kissed the top of her head.

Jonah sat down next to them with Frankie in his arms. "This little guy's almost out," he said. "How's Jolie holding up?"

Diane smiled lovingly at the baby next to her. "She's been asleep since you left."

"Guess it's time to get these kiddos to bed." Jonah shifted Frankie up onto his shoulder and started to stand.

"I don't want to go to bed," Pippa mumbled.

Frankie yawned and burrowed deeper into Jonah's shoulder. "Me neither."

"Tell you what." Diane got to her feet. "I'll put Jolie down while you guys stay up a little longer."

Kenzie tried to stand, but the weight of Pippa on her lap kept her seated. "No, I need to…"

"Don't be silly." Grabbing the handle of Jolie's carrier, Diane shot Kenzie a conspiratorial look. "Enjoy the last little bit of the fire." With that, she headed up the porch steps and disappeared into the house.

Kenzie stared into the glowing orange embers, trying not to focus on the thought that she was holding Jonah's first child on her lap, while right next to her he was holding the little brother Pippa had always wanted. The idea made her heart ache, made her want to ask the man sitting beside her if he'd gotten her messages all those years ago.

But her—*their*—little girl was fast asleep now, and the last thing Kenzie wanted to do was wake her up. So she let a few minutes pass in silence, then sniffed back her tears and shoved down her questions before turning to Jonah. "She's fallen asleep. I'd better take her inside."

He gave her a regretful shrug. "Yeah, this little guy's down for the count, too. Guess we wore them out." He grinned. "At least they should sleep well, huh?"

They both rose at the same time. Jonah went ahead and opened the door to the house, then the door to her apartment so she wouldn't have to let go of Pippa. With a nod of thanks, Kenzie slipped inside. He closed the door gently behind her.

As she changed her sleeping child into a nightie, Kenzie kept wondering why Jonah hadn't called her the second he read the final letter. The secret Diane had shared with her had revived all those feelings of hurt and resentment. In all of her messages, Kenzie had apologized, said she wanted to come back to Boston and be with him again. He'd been so heartbroken by the breakup she felt sure he'd be thrilled to have her back. She'd waited and waited, her hope waning with every passing hour.

His lack of response spoke louder than any words, especially given the contents of her last letter. Or so it seemed at the time. But maybe there was something else behind his silence. Elena had made no secret of her dislike of Kenzie, and according to Jonah, she'd jumped in as soon as Kenzie was gone.

Could Elena have intercepted Kenzie's messages and gotten rid of them before Jonah could see them?

Even if she had, how on earth could Kenzie ask Jonah about it? Grilling him about his late wife's possible duplicity sounded like a terrible thing to do. He clearly loved Elena and was still grieving her.

But if that was what had happened, it meant Jonah hadn't simply ignored Kenzie.

And it meant he had no idea Pippa was his child.

With a sigh of frustration, Kenzie tucked Pippa in and kissed her forehead. "Night, sweet girl," she whispered before tiptoeing out of the room.

But she couldn't settle down. If she sat on the sofa, she sprang up again a second later and sat in one of the chairs. If she turned on the TV, all she did was flip unseeing through the channels. She thought about going to bed but knew she'd just end up lying there wide awake.

Finally she strode outside to the back porch, figuring she could look at the stars and pray for peace. Pippa's window faced the porch and was open enough that Kenzie would hear if she called out. That seemed unlikely, given what a sound sleeper Pippa was.

Back in the cool night air, Kenzie leaned against a column next to the porch steps and looked up at the sky. The sheer number of stars took her breath away. It was impossible to see them in the city, where the glaring lights obscured them. But out here in the country they filled the heavens on a clear night like this one, and they actually seemed to sparkle.

As she studied them in breathless wonder, Kenzie felt peace wash through her heart and soul. *Thank You, dear Lord, for this wonderful new home*, she prayed silently.

"Beautiful, isn't it?"

Kenzie almost jumped out of her skin at the voice behind her. She stifled a shriek so she wouldn't wake Pippa and whirled around to find Jonah sitting on the porch swing. "I—I didn't see you there!" she stammered.

He got up and moved toward her, standing next to her at the top of the steps and gazing upward. "Sorry. Didn't expect anyone to join me. I come out here a lot at night, just to look at the sky. The kids' rooms are right there, so I can hear if they call."

He was standing so close to Kenzie she could feel the warmth coming from him. Maybe because of the questions she'd been entertaining a few moments ago, she felt differently toward Jonah. Something she should know better than to feel for this man.

She tried to move away without being too obvious about it, but the porch post was in the way. She could either go down the steps into the darkness or walk backward to get to the door, which would look silly. So she stayed put, filled with conflicting emotions, her arms folded across her chest like a protective barrier.

Finally she dredged up what seemed like an appropriate response, awkwardly indicating the window behind her. "Pippa's room is right there, too." *Your other daughter*, she added silently.

He didn't respond for a moment, just stood there staring up at the starry canopy. "Seemed like she had a good time tonight."

Despite her discomfort, Kenzie couldn't suppress a smile at the memory of her daughter's happiness. "She had a ball. Guess she's a country mouse at heart." She stopped herself before she could add, *Just like her father*.

"Wonder where she gets that from?" Jonah chuckled.

Kenzie turned her head and studied him, looking for some kind of sign that he knew he was Pippa's father. His face showed only humor and kindness. Perplexed, Kenzie turned her gaze back to the heavens. "I'm sure I have no idea."

"I'm impressed with how much you've taken to country living." Jonah seemed oblivious to her confusion. "I wasn't sure you'd be able to stick it out, given how squeamish you were during that camping trip we took."

Kenzie whipped her head around in surprise. She could feel her face heating up with embarrassment. "Um…"

It was obvious that Jonah realized he'd made a mistake. He scrunched up his face. "I'm sorry. I…I guess maybe you'd rather forget that trip."

Kenzie kept her eyes glued to his face until he looked at her. Despite the darkness, she could see the blush cover his cheeks as that night in the tent came back to him.

"Kenz… I'm such an idiot. I'm so sorry." He took her by the wrist. "Please forgive me."

She peered up at him, trying to figure out how to react, but the mournful brown eyes looking down at her dissolved her confusion. All she could think of was how much she'd loved him all those years ago, and how foolish she'd been to end things the way she did.

She'd been furious that he hadn't proposed after what happened on the camping trip. Instead, he'd run off to spend a week with his mother and had hardly been in touch with Kenzie. She'd felt ignored, rejected. The hurt festered out of proportion until he returned. Then she'd said mean, ugly things that she couldn't unsay. In just a few minutes she'd destroyed what they had. Maybe she had a few things to apologize for as well.

Jonah was still holding on to her wrist, his face wistful and tender. Suddenly Kenzie couldn't bear to look at him for another second. But instead of looking away, she fell forward against him, burying her face in his chest.

Mistake.

The scent of him, the warmth of him, the sensation of his heart pounding next to her ear, all filled her with a rush of regret. She knew she should pull away, but something kept her from moving a muscle. All she could do was rest against him and wish she could go back eight years.

After a stunned moment, she felt Jonah's arms creep around her and pull her closer. Kenzie didn't resist. She still couldn't move. She just wanted to sink into this sweet, comforting moment and stay there.

"Kenzie," Jonah whispered into her hair. He pulled back slightly and put a finger under her chin, lifting her head so they could look at each other.

Kenzie held her breath and gazed steadily at that face, once the dearest thing in the world to her. Too much time had passed since they'd been this close. His thick brown hair had more than a few silver threads, his laugh lines had deepened, but he was still the man she'd been sure she was going to marry.

And whether he knew it or not, she'd had his child. That was a bond like no other.

Jonah stroked her cheek, tucked a curl behind her ear. "Kenzie," he said again, "I…"

An ear-shattering shriek pierced the silence, followed by a series of little screams and hysterical sobbing. Kenzie jumped a mile, but Jonah steadied her with his firm hand and spoke quickly. "Frankie. He's having night terrors."

He was gone like a shot, leaving Kenzie breathless on the porch, feeling as if she'd been turned inside out.

"What frightened you, buddy? Was it another bad dream?"

Although he was deeply disappointed at having his moment with Kenzie interrupted, Jonah wasn't sorry to be holding his son and comforting him. These days, anything that strengthened their tenuous connection was precious, even if it was a nightmare.

"There was a bad man," Frankie choked out. "He wanted to hurt Mommy."

"That is scary." Knowing his naturally loud voice sometimes frightened the boy, Jonah focused on keeping his tone low and calming. "But it was just a dream, right?"

Frankie whimpered and sniffled. "I don't know. He was mad at Mommy and was yelling at her real loud."

Jonah hugged his son more tightly. "You know a man didn't hurt Mommy, don't you?"

The boy looked up at him with huge, terrified eyes. "It wasn't Mommy Elena. It was my real mommy."

Jonah had to grit his teeth and push down anger against his late wife for telling their son he wasn't really their child. She'd done it soon after Jolena was born, probably already under the influence of postpartum depression and pain medication. But why she'd done it at all confounded Jonah. They'd discussed telling Frankie at some point, but not when he was only five years old and still fragile from his early trauma. Unfortunately, Frankie hadn't mentioned it to Jonah until after Elena's death, so he couldn't ask her what she'd been thinking.

Forcing himself to go still inside, Jonah met his son's gaze. "Do you remember your real mommy?"

Frankie's eyebrows met in a confused arch. "I don't know. Sometimes. Did she have kind of yellow hair like Miss Thorsen at school?"

Jonah held his breath. Lana Tiffman had had unnaturally blond hair with several inches of dark roots. The long, scraggly tresses had spread out around her head like a halo as she lay unresponsive next to her hysterical toddler. Did the boy actually have that memory? He'd only been two years old at the time, but it was possible.

Had the memories just started coming back to Frankie? Was that the reason for his recent regression?

"Yes, buddy. She had yellow hair."

"Why was the bad man yelling so loud?"

"I don't know, son. But he shouldn't have been yelling. I'm sorry he scared you."

But he couldn't help mulling over Frankie's nightmare.

Although he'd left the force well over a year ago, being a cop was still in Jonah's blood.

As her death had presented more like an overdose than a murder, the investigation into Lana Tiffman's demise had been cursory. Had there been a "bad man" that two-year-old Frankie saw yelling at his mother? If so, did he have anything to do with Lana's death? And could he possibly have been Frankie's father?

But what was the point of all these questions? No one they'd spoken to had any idea who Lana's boyfriend or Frankie's father was. According to the neighbors, she had lots of male friends. No policeman in his right mind would ask to reopen the investigation based on a traumatized little boy's nightmare.

No point in thinking about that right now. Jonah kissed the top of Frankie's head and tucked him back under the covers. Once his son had drifted back to sleep, Jonah tiptoed out of the bedroom to sit in his recliner and relive that sweet, brief moment with Kenzie.

A soft tap on the door roused him from his thoughts. His heart filled with hope that it was Kenzie, Jonah launched himself from the chair and opened the door.

His face must have registered his disappointment, because Diane laughed as she stepped inside. "Hoping I was your other neighbor, were you?"

Jonah gave his sister a rueful shrug. "Am I that transparent?"

They headed to the area by the fireplace and sat side by side on the sofa. "I saw some sparks tonight that weren't from the bonfire," Diane chuckled. "And now you're blushing." When he didn't laugh, she added, "I guess I shouldn't tease you."

He stood abruptly and walked to the fireplace, looking at the photos on the mantelpiece. Most were pictures of himself, Elena and Frankie. There was only a single photo of Jolena, taken at the hospital shortly after she'd left the NICU. He hadn't wanted a picture of her in the incubator, hooked up to all kinds of scary contraptions. The difficult labor and birth had nearly killed both mother and child, but excellent medical care had brought them through.

When they got home, Elena refused to let him take pictures of her with the baby, claiming she was fat and ugly. Despite the fulfillment of her long-held wish of motherhood, she didn't dote on Jolena, didn't interact with her the way a new mother usually did. She saw to the baby's needs in an almost robotic fashion. She'd practically ignored Frankie, who thought she'd suddenly stopped loving him because of the baby. Jonah had chalked Elena's behavior up to the aftereffects of the traumatic birth and the anesthetic they'd given her for the emergency C-section.

He should have paid more attention. He should have asked questions. He should have taken her to see someone.

He should have known something was very, very wrong.

"You must miss her terribly."

Diane's words jarred him. He'd almost forgotten she was there. "Of course I miss her. And so do the kids."

"I heard Frankie screaming a little while ago. That seems to be happening more often lately."

With a sigh, Jonah sank back onto the sofa. "The nightmares are back and they're escalating. I don't know why."

"Do you know what they're about?"

Covering his face with his hands, Jonah shook his head. "He says it's about his real mom and some bad man who hurt her. He was only a toddler but I suppose it's possible."

Diane leaned back, a worried expression on her face. "So much for a little guy to handle, losing two mothers. It's no wonder he's afraid he'll be abandoned."

Jonah sat very still for a moment, head in hands. Finally, in a very soft voice, he said, "It's my fault she died."

"What?" Diane's disbelief was clear in her sharp response.

He dragged himself to a more upright position, guilt gnawing at his stomach. "I should have known something was wrong. She wasn't acting like herself. Of course, I knew she was on medication, but I never imagined she'd take it, then leave the kids alone and go for a drive."

He felt his sister's hand on his shoulder. "You were working a ton of hours and picking up the slack with the kids while Elena recovered."

Jonah closed his eyes and grimaced at the memory. "I should have taken more family medical leave so I could keep a better eye on things while she healed. She seemed calmer, so I thought she was getting better, not worse."

Diane squeezed his shoulder. "Maybe she thought she was getting better, too. You know she hated to worry you."

"I should have noticed how she was neglecting Frankie." He turned miserable, haunted eyes to his sister. "That was completely out of character. And she started snapping at me, which she'd never done before. But I chalked it up to what she'd just been through."

"That's surprising," Diane admitted. "I'd never seen a woman so in love, even the first time I met her, before you met Kenzie." When Jonah shot her a questioning look, she continued. "Just before I left for Haiti, remember? I came to Boston to stay with you and we all had dinner together. I could tell she was totally smitten but was doing her best to keep things professional." Diane gave her brother a reproving shake of the head. "Next thing I knew, you were raving about this little redhead."

Jonah slumped against the back of the sofa, processing the information his sister had just given him. "That far back? Really?"

"I had a feeling you were oblivious." Diane grinned. "I'm sure Elena was relieved once Kenzie was out of the picture."

He mulled over Diane's revelation. "She started hanging around a lot right after Kenzie left, making sure I was okay.

I was a mess for a while. I got the feeling she was trying to protect me, in some way."

"Yeah, you were a barrel of laughs. But Elena was great. I was thrilled when you finally realized what a wonderful person she was. I was over the moon when you got married and took Frankie in." Diane's sigh was weighted with sorrow. "I never imagined it would end so tragically."

Jonah slung an arm around his sister and pulled her close. "Did I ever tell you she's the one who proposed?"

Diane laughed. "No, but I'm not surprised to hear it. That girl knew what she wanted and made no bones about going for it."

Despite the subject, Jonah felt himself smiling. "Yup, that was Elena. She didn't exactly ask me to marry her—she told me to. Said we were great together, and if we got married, we'd have a better chance of adopting Frankie." His voice thickened. "Said she liked me enough to put up with me for the rest of her life."

"Oh, Jonah," Diane breathed. "Don't make me cry."

"Within a year we were fostering Frankie and starting the adoption process. Then she was pregnant." Overwhelmed just thinking about everything that had happened, he blinked and shook his head rapidly. "Then…"

Diane wrapped her arm around her brother's shoulders. "No one could have predicted that Elena would try to drive after taking opioids. I mean, she was a former cop. She knew what that stuff could do."

"But I should have noticed. I could have done something."

Diane embraced her brother as his body went rigid with the effort of holding back tears. "You can't blame yourself, sweetie," she pleaded.

After a moment he pulled away. "But I have to be honest with myself." Jonah rubbed his eyes on his sleeve and cleared his throat. "So please don't expect me to move on or encourage me to think about Kenzie again. I know that's what you were doing tonight, leaving us together by the bonfire."

Diane shook her head in violent disagreement. "But—"

"But nothing." Jonah glanced back toward the hallway where the kids' bedrooms were. "I need to focus on my children. It's what Elena would have wanted." With a sad smile he added, "And having put me back together after the breakup, she definitely would not have wanted me to go chasing after Kenzie Reid again."

Chapter Seven

The moment on the porch with Jonah had left Kenzie dazed. After he ran inside to take care of Frankie, she wandered back into her apartment in a stupor, bewildered by what had happened, by her involuntary display of vulnerability.

It almost seemed as if Jonah had wanted to kiss her.

And maybe she had wanted him to.

Despite all of her long-term anger, she'd practically fallen into Jonah Raymond's arms. And it had happened only a few feet from their sleeping daughter's bedroom window.

The daughter he still hadn't acknowledged.

Why wasn't she furious with him or with herself? Instead, she was moping around reliving that moment and hoping for more.

And what would have happened if Frankie hadn't had a nightmare?

Kenzie found herself blushing. Even though no one was there to witness the extent of her stupidity, she collapsed in an embarrassed heap on the sofa and buried her face in the cushions.

Maybe it was time to mend things instead of pretending they'd never happened.

As soon as that thought crossed her mind, she stomped on it as if it were a cockroach. Okay, so they'd embraced. It had been quick, meaningless. Right?

But it sure hadn't felt meaningless. The moment had been fraught with complex emotions.

She couldn't reach back eight years and prevent herself from getting so worked up she couldn't think straight, but she could stop being such a coward and tell the poor guy exactly why she'd broken up with him. In retrospect her reasoning seemed childish, rooted in hurt pride. Right after their camping trip he'd gone to see his family for a week and had hardly been in touch with her. She was still reeling from what had happened and interpreted his withdrawal as a loss of interest in her.

But what if he actually didn't want to interrupt her while she was studying? He'd known she was going to have an exceptionally busy, intense week. What if he was just trying to give her space?

There was still the question of why he hadn't responded to her frantic emails and letters. But what if he hadn't read them?

What if he had no idea he was Pippa's father?

Kenzie suddenly realized she was pacing her apartment, excited by the thought of resolving long-buried problems. She would ask Jonah why he'd never responded to all her apologies, requests to get back together, and finally her pregnancy. Maybe that would make him realize that Kenzie regretted her abrupt end to their relationship.

Kenzie knew she had to talk to Jonah. The sooner the better.

Since Holiday Farm was closed on Sunday, Jonah and Diane bundled the children into her car and headed to church. Jonah noted that Kenzie's car was gone and wondered if he'd see her there. He'd been avoiding her since their embrace on Friday night, which wasn't hard because the farm was overrun with apple pickers all day Saturday.

Sure enough, when they pulled into the parking lot, Kenzie's station wagon was already there. He and Diane noticed it at the same time and exchanged a glance.

"Everything okay with you two?" Diane asked. "You've been a bit distracted."

Jonah sighed and shook his head. "Everything's fine." He turned to the back seat. "Okay, Frankie, unbuckle your sister." When Frankie obeyed without objection, Jonah sighed again, this time with relief.

In the sunlit sanctuary, Jonah immediately spotted Kenzie's and Pippa's curly mops, shiny copper and bright strawberry blond side by side in a pew near the back. As Diane took the kids to the Sunday school room, Jonah debated the wisdom of going up to them after the resolution he'd made Friday night. Fortunately, his dilemma was interrupted by Enid and her husband, Pastor Mullin.

"Jonah! How wonderful to see you here again." Enid embraced him warmly with her long arms.

"Welcome back, son." The stout little pastor gave him a firm handshake, grinning from ear to ear. "We've missed you, as I'm sure my beautiful wife let you know."

Cheered by their sincere greeting, Jonah returned their smiles. "It's time to get our lives back on track."

"You picked a good place to start, if I do say so myself." Pastor Mullin chuckled, and then his face grew serious. "How's little Frankie doing these days?"

"He's up and down," Jonah admitted. "I never know what to expect."

Enid nodded, her face solemn. "You're doing a wonderful job, Jonah. I can't imagine how hard it must be."

Pastor Mullin's iron gray eyebrows furrowed with concern. "It's a very heavy burden to bear, but you know we're here to help whenever we can. Please don't hesitate to call on us."

Jonah felt his throat tighten with gratitude. "Thanks, both of you," he whispered.

"We should have him over to dinner, don't you think?" Enid asked her husband.

"Absolutely. Especially if that means you'll make your wonderful stew," Pastor Mullin added with a mischievous grin. "With lots of biscuits, of course."

"Oh, you." Enid gave her husband a playful push, then noticed Kenzie and her daughter sitting nearby. "Henry, that's our new arts teacher. We'd better go say hello before you take the pulpit." She beamed at Jonah. "I'll get back to you about dinner. Maybe this week?" When Jonah nodded, she and the pastor hurried away to greet Kenzie.

Suddenly feeling melancholy, Jonah watched them talk to Kenzie and Pippa. The Mullins were the happiest couple he'd ever known, married over forty years and still apparently in love and content. He'd thought he and Elena had a shot at something like that, even though he hadn't been in love with her at first.

Love grew. Then she was gone.

Before Elena, he'd been sure he'd found the love of his life in Kenzie. Then that camping trip seemed to ruin everything.

If only she'd talked to him about what had upset her so much, instead of breaking up with him. He'd gone to see his mother to tell her he wanted to marry Kenzie, and to get the antique engagement ring that had belonged to his grandmother. It had been in his pocket while Kenzie stomped around and told him she was moving to the other side of the country. Instead of a fiancée, he'd gotten a broken heart.

"Penny for them." Diane appeared at his elbow. "And if you stare any harder at Kenzie, you might set her on fire."

Ignoring her comments, Jonah headed for the pew on the other side of the aisle from Kenzie. Pippa jumped up and ran off, presumably to go to Sunday school. Frankie would be happy to have her there.

Jonah sighed as he opened his hymnal. Maybe he should

confront Kenzie instead of avoiding her. Maybe it was time for him to ask what had happened eight years ago that made her break his heart without warning.

Would she tell him the truth?

There was only one way to find out.

After the service, the congregation gathered in the large fellowship hall for coffee and treats. Kenzie and Pippa found themselves surrounded by friendly faces welcoming them, Pastor and Dr. Mullin the friendliest.

Enid enfolded Kenzie in her arms, then pulled away to beam at her. "I'm so pleased to see you two in our flock!"

Beaming back, Kenzie exclaimed, "It was a lovely service! I've never been to such a spirited church."

The pastor threw back his head and laughed. "We do love to sing to the Lord, at the tops of our lungs."

"We sang a bunch in Sunday school, too," Pippa said eagerly. "It was so much fun. Can we come back, Mommy?" Standing next to Pippa, Frankie studied her curiously but didn't say anything. Pippa seized his hand. "Frankie's too shy to sing, but I think he should do it anyway because it's fun."

Kenzie hadn't noticed Jonah standing behind Frankie until he spoke. "That was a wonderful message, Pastor. And one I needed to hear."

The pastor nodded. "We all need to be reminded of the two greatest commandments now and then. If you love God with all your heart, loving your neighbor comes naturally."

Kenzie glanced at Jonah to find him looking at her. Blushing, she looked away.

Enid was patting her husband's arm. "Yes, dear, we don't need an encore," she laughed. Turning to Kenzie, she said, "We'd love to have you over to dinner some night this week. How's Wednesday?"

"That sounds great," Kenzie agreed happily.

Pastor Mullin's eyes lit up. "Before the service we were talking about having Jonah and his brood over. Maybe we could have a little dinner party!"

Kenzie thought she caught an uneasy look on Enid's face at her husband's suggestion, but it vanished quickly. "Of course! That's a wonderful idea." She smiled at Jonah. "We'll make it nice and early for the children, of course. Five o'clock?"

Jonah glanced worriedly at Kenzie before saying, "Okay. Yes. We'll be there."

Chapter Eight

That afternoon, Kenzie was trying to relax on the back porch swing as she geared herself up for talking to Jonah. Half of her was watching Pippa and Frankie play a hilarious two-person version of softball that involved making up a lot of rules on the spot. The other half still hadn't stopped reliving Friday night's encounter.

What had she been thinking?

Truth was, she hadn't been thinking. Not at all. If she had, there was no way she would have let herself literally fall into his arms. But that didn't stop her heart from fluttering like a fledgling bird when she thought back to that night: the sky crammed full of shimmering stars, Jonah standing close beside her, waves of nostalgia washing through her.

Why had she given in to her emotions and leaned against him? Why hadn't she said good-night and gone inside like a sane human being? Now she had not only those treacherous old feelings to contend with, but also a fresh memory of being in his embrace again.

And she'd talked herself into having a very difficult conversation with him. She knew she had to do it as soon as possible, before she lost her nerve.

Next to her head she heard the screen door creak open. Kenzie's radar was so tuned up she knew it was Jonah without even looking. His voice, gentled down from its full power, confirmed it.

"Hey."

When he sat next to her without asking, Kenzie sat up straight and almost ran away. A big hand on her arm stopped her. "Please don't leave."

Looking at him was a terrible idea, but Kenzie made herself turn her head. There he was in jeans and a sweatshirt, holding little Jolie to his shoulder as she slept. It was way too adorable, designed to make a woman melt, so she cranked up her inner icebox and forced out the most dreaded words in the English language.

"We need to talk."

Jonah groaned. "What have I done now?"

Kenzie scrambled to find a good answer but couldn't come up with a thing. "N-nothing," she stammered. "It's just…"

"We hugged," Jonah finished for her. "Right over there, a couple of nights ago."

"I know, but—"

"Don't worry about it."

That was not the response she'd been expecting, and it made what she'd planned to say feel even more awkward and out of place. "Don't worry about it?" she echoed lamely.

Rubbing Jolie's back, he nodded. "It was a mistake. It won't happen again. So please don't yell at me." He gave her a whimsical grin that softened his words a bit.

Thoroughly confused, Kenzie blinked at him. "O…kay."

"You're right. It's a bad idea. We're both completely different people now, and we have other things to think about." He gave her a knowing side-glance. "That's more or less what you were going to say, right?"

"Um…" He was completely wrong, but Kenzie couldn't find the words to set him straight. "Yeah, I guess."

"Great!" Jonah sat there a moment longer, looking as if he had more to say. But Jolie stirred in her sleep, then opened her big brown eyes and smiled at her father. Jonah smiled back and kissed the tip of her nose, apparently forgetting Kenzie's existence.

Bewildered, Kenzie got up from the porch swing and went inside, back to the comfort of her apartment. Keeping her eye on the kids through the picture window, she curled up on the sofa and picked up her reverie where Jonah had interrupted it.

But he hadn't just interrupted it, had he? He'd completely changed the tone of her thinking with that "don't worry about it" remark. She'd been trying to figure out how to tell him she'd made a mistake all those years ago, and ask him why he'd ignored her urgent, apologetic messages.

Now she was upset that he'd told her their brief embrace was a mistake.

Shouldn't she be relieved? Yes, she should. But she wasn't. Instead, her feelings were hurt.

What was wrong with her? How could she possibly still have feelings for Jonah? Again she reminded herself that after their camping trip, he'd run off to his family the next day. She'd hardly heard from him for days. What kind of guy did that?

Sighing, Kenzie forced herself to be honest. She'd known he was close to his widowed mother and visited her as often as possible. And he tended to get busy with fixing things for her and spending time with his family and old friends when he was there. He was probably too distracted to think much about what had happened that weekend.

But to Kenzie it had felt like desertion. She'd fervently hoped that when Jonah returned, he'd propose. Especially after she told him about the job in San Franciso that she'd accepted. It was the best offer she'd received by far, an exceptional position for someone just out of grad school. She would have been a fool to turn it down.

Jonah hadn't proposed. Even when she suggested they both might relocate to San Francisco. Together. Hint, hint.

Nope. Jonah had given her the basset-hound eyes and said, "Kenz, you know I need to stay around New England. I want to be near my family."

Kenzie's heart broke and her feelings of hurt and rejection had taken over. Without waiting to hear another word, she'd shut him down and flown off to the West Coast, vowing never to speak to Jonah Raymond again. He'd blown it. His loss.

Then, a few weeks after her move, nausea and fatigue hit. The home pregnancy test came up positive and was confirmed by a doctor.

When Jonah ghosted her, marrying Greg Halloran had seemed like the best choice. He was a good guy, he adored her, and she enjoyed his company. They worked together in the studio and it turned out he was behind her landing the job of her dreams. Shortly after they'd moved back to Boston, the weird symptoms hit. Kenzie had felt so sick she couldn't function well, could barely think straight. No doctor she saw could tell her what was wrong. Every one of them referred her to someone else who couldn't tell her what was wrong. She ended up with diagnoses of fibromyalgia, chronic fatigue and migraines. The only treatments they recommended were pain medications, which she refused to take.

She lost her job. She lost three babies. Then Greg had confessed he was in love with someone else, and she was pregnant. He wanted a divorce so he could marry Camilla.

Kenzie yanked her mind back to the present. She had traveled way too far down a dark road. Time to take some positive steps.

She'd promised Pippa that she'd invite Greg to visit once they were settled. Pushing herself upright, Kenzie grabbed her laptop and typed an email to invite her ex to Chapelton some weekend afternoon. She knew he was wrapped up in his new wife and offspring-to-be, but surely he could spend a few hours visiting the little girl he'd helped Kenzie raise even though she wasn't his own.

Kenzie hoped so, anyway. If the disconnect went on much longer, Pippa would be hurt. Greg had never been Father of the Year, but he was the only father her daughter had ever known. As little as Kenzie wanted to see her ex, there was nothing she wouldn't do for Pippa.

The thoughts made her wonder how Pippa would react if she knew Jonah was her real father. Shocked, no doubt, and full of potentially embarrassing questions. But she seemed to like Jonah, and she definitely adored Frankie and Jolie. What if…?

Kenzie shook herself, finished the email and sent it to Greg. Despite that sweet moment they'd shared the other night, Jonah had made it clear that it had meant nothing.

And wasn't that what she'd told him she wanted?

If Jonah had made up his mind for sure that holding Kenzie in his arms would never happen again, why did he feel so miserable about it?

He'd thought he was saying what he'd decided to say to Kenzie. He'd thought he was saying what she wanted him to say. Given her determination to avoid him, surely she'd want to pretend that embrace had never happened. And given all the things he'd told himself, he wanted to forget it as well.

Didn't he?

"Da! Da! Da! Da!"

Jolie's insistent cries to get his attention finally penetrated Jonah's emotional fog. He got back to spooning lunch into her food-smeared face as she slapped at the high chair tray, spraying peas and carrots in all directions.

Frankie spoke from one side of his mouth, like a gangster. "She's gross."

Jonah started to correct his son but stopped himself. "Yeah, she can be kind of messy," he agreed. "But that's because she's just a baby."

"And she stinks." Frankie demonstrated his point by holding his nose.

Jonah frowned at his son. "That isn't a very nice thing to say."

"You always say to be honest."

Jonah took a breath and thought carefully before responding in a level, kind tone. "But we think before we speak, right, buddy? We don't say something hurtful even if we think it's the truth."

"She can't understand what anyone is saying, so it doesn't hurt her." Frankie took a bite of his grilled cheese sandwich. "I bet Pippa doesn't get in trouble for saying things like that."

Mentally counting to ten, Jonah told himself to respond calmly. Frankie was sometimes startled by Jonah's naturally loud voice, so he'd been making an effort to speak more softly. "That's up to Pippa's mother, Frankie. And maybe Jolie stinks sometimes, but again, she's just a baby."

Frankie scowled. "Jolie gets away with everything because she's a baby. It's not fair."

In spite of himself, Jonah smiled at the boy's observation. "Maybe it doesn't seem fair, but she really is too little to help it."

"I bet if I threw my food all over the place and made a mess in my pants, I'd get in trouble."

Jonah chuckled and tousled his son's hair. "I'd be disappointed because you're a big boy and know better. But when you were Jolie's age, you were pretty gross, too."

Frankie jerked away. If his lower lip stuck out any farther, it would be resting on the table. He glared at his father. "Pippa says she's always wanted a little brother and she's going to ask her mommy if they can 'dopt me."

Despite the hurt that knifed his heart, Jonah kept his face as neutral as he could manage. "Don't you want me to be your daddy anymore?"

Frankie's eyes filled with tears, making Jonah realize that this acting-out came from a place of pain, not anger. "I don't like when you shout."

"Do you think I shout a lot?" Jonah couldn't keep the surprise out of his tone. He'd been so careful to speak gently to Frankie, although at times his frustration broke through. "Buddy, you know I have a loud voice. Do you think I'm mad at you?"

Frankie scrubbed his eyes with his palms. "Sometimes. It's scary."

"I'm sorry, son. I don't mean to be scary." Jonah frantically tried to think back to the last time he'd been angry with Frankie. "I was a policeman and sometimes I had to yell to stop the bad guys. Now I teach in a gym, which also means I have to yell just to be heard. But I'm not being loud because I'm angry, okay? I'm just…loud."

"It sounds like yelling." Frankie crossed his arms and furrowed his brow.

"I'm sorry," Jonah repeated. "I honestly don't mean to yell or make you think I'm angry." He felt his throat close as he pushed his chair closer to Frankie, leaving Jolie to grind the rest of her lunch into the tray. "I love you, son. I hope you know that."

But when he tried to put an arm around the boy, Frankie drew back. "I'm not your son."

"Frankie," Jonah choked out.

"Do you know who my real daddy is?"

So many emotions were swirling around inside Jonah that he felt off-balance. Frankie's words winded him as if he'd been punched in the stomach.

Jonah took an extra deep breath to quell the pain in his chest and spoke as gently as he could. "Don't you want me to adopt you anymore?"

The little boy's eyebrows furrowed as tears spilled down his cheeks. He sniffled furiously. "I want to be Pippa's little brother."

Tamping down the heartache, Jonah tried to hug Frankie again. To his relief, the boy didn't pull away this time, although he tensed up a bit. "Pippa may not be your big sister, but she's your best friend, isn't she?"

Frankie nodded and sniffled again. "But if you married Pippa's mommy, she'd be my big sister for real."

Jonah didn't know whether to laugh or cry, so he hugged his son closer.

Chapter Nine

"**M**ommy, come *on*!"

Pippa's exasperated cry didn't help at all. Kenzie stood at the bottom of the outdoor stairs that led to the parsonage, one foot on the first step, hand gripping the banister. Try as she might, she was finding it hard to overcome the headache and vertigo enough to take another step.

"In a minute, baby girl." She hoped her reassuring tone masked her uncertainty. "I might have left something behind in the car."

"What?" Pippa demanded. "I have the pie."

"I'm trying to think." Kenzie looked up at her impatient daughter and pushed a smile onto her face. "Why don't you go ahead? I'll catch up with you once I've checked, okay?"

Her daughter didn't need further encouragement. She flew up the last few steps, holding the blueberry pie at a dangerous angle, and knocked on the parsonage door. When it opened, she announced, "Mommy's coming! She might have forgot something, so she has to think about it."

Once Pippa had squeezed through, Pastor Mullin waved from the doorway and called out, "Is there anything I can help with, dear heart?"

Warmed by his kindness, Kenzie replied with a smile, "Nope, all good! Just left something in the car. I'll be right there!"

The pastor nodded and stepped back into the parsonage. Trying to appear casual, Kenzie went back to the car, opened her purse and took out the untouched bottle of painkillers. She'd tossed the vial in her purse as an afterthought because of the persistent headache. Would taking half of one make it possible for her to get through the evening without betraying how much her head hurt?

But she hadn't overcome her trepidation about taking the pain medication. Throughout her athletic years she'd been a big advocate of "walk it off." Although "walking it off" didn't seem even remotely possible at the moment. With grim determination, she put the vial back in her purse and took two aspirin instead.

Two aspirin. Years ago, just one used to make her fall asleep. She hoped Enid had made a big pot of strong coffee.

It would take at least twenty minutes for the aspirin to kick in, but she could fake it in the meantime. Determined, she got out of the car and put her foot on the bottom step again.

Taking a deep breath and blowing it out slowly, Kenzie grasped the banister tightly with both hands and pulled herself up to the next step. Then the next, going hand over hand, pausing on each step to rest, coaching herself under her breath—*you can do this, you're fine, everything's fine*. Finally she reached the top.

On the porch she took a moment to compose herself. Lately she'd been having more trouble managing stairs, among other things. Her head spun if she moved too quickly, and the fatigue never seemed to let up.

Every symptom she looked up pointed to Lyme disease, in spite of what the Boston doctors and tests said. She knew the pain couldn't possibly be in her imagination or caused by depression. She knew what depression felt like, having suffered from it after every miscarriage. Yes, it was exhausting and it could make you ache, but what Kenzie was dealing with now went way beyond what emotional pain had done to her.

She wasn't sick because she was depressed. She was depressed because she was sick.

"Hey, everything okay?"

Kenzie jumped at the sound of the voice in front of her. She'd been holding on to the railing with her eyes closed, completely distracted by how she felt, and hadn't heard Jonah open the parsonage door. When she tried to look up at him, her neck spasmed and she gasped at the sudden, stabbing pain. But she still managed to smile. "Yup, everything's just fine."

Joining her on the porch, Jonah studied her, clearly unconvinced. "You look like you're in pain again."

Kenzie lifted a shoulder, trying to appear carefree. "Nope, absolutely fine. Did Pippa get the pie there in one piece?"

She let go of the railing and took a step but couldn't suppress a wince as her head throbbed. Jonah was at her side in an instant, taking her arm and peering into her face with deep concern. "You are not fine, by any stretch of the imagination."

As the pain calmed down, she tried to laugh it off. "It was just a little twinge."

Jonah shook his head. "Don't forget, I know you. I've seen you keep smiling right after you pulled a muscle. What's going on, Kenz?"

"Is she okay?" A booming voice came from behind Jonah as a substantial, bearded man stepped out of the door and onto the porch. "Did she hurt herself?" The man shouldered Jonah aside to take a closer look. "I'm Diane's husband, by the way. Dr. Paul Solomon. And you must be Kenzie."

Struggling to appear normal, Kenzie spoke in a bright tone. "I know Diane was off to pick you up at Logan, but I had no idea you'd be here tonight. You must be tired after such a long flight!"

"I'm just fine," Paul said, "but you don't look like you're doing so well."

"She's in pain a lot," Jonah explained. "But she won't say what it is, other than headaches."

Paul frowned. "Does she have a headache? Could it be a migraine?"

Kenzie scowled at the men hovering over her. "Hello? I'm right here. I can answer any questions you may have about my okay-ness."

"Yes, but will you answer them truthfully?"

Jonah's tone pushed the wrong buttons, putting Kenzie on the defensive. "Even if I do, will you believe me, or will you decide you know better?"

Paul gave Jonah a wry smile. "Maybe you should go back inside," he advised. "Leave the medical stuff to me."

With another glance at Kenzie, Jonah shrugged. "I'm only worried about you, Kenzie, because you don't seem to be getting better. In fact, if anything, you seem worse." He turned and disappeared into the parsonage.

"Have you seen a doctor about this?" Paul spoke to Kenzie directly this time.

"I've seen just about every doctor in the world over the past two years," she admitted.

He smiled sympathetically. "Well, there's one doctor you haven't seen."

Puzzled, she shook her head. "I didn't mean it literally, but…who?"

"Me."

Kenzie balked. "I'd rather not see someone I know."

He nodded his shaggy head. "I get it, but—well, not to be immodest, I'm one heck of a diagnostician. And even more importantly, I listen to my patients."

Still unwilling to agree, Kenzie didn't have the energy to argue. "I'll think about it," she lied. "Right now we should get inside, shouldn't we?"

The sumptuous meal was over in less than an hour. Now they all lay around the comfortable living room, stuffed and groaning, protesting that they couldn't possibly even think about having dessert.

The evening might have gotten off to a rocky start health-wise, but the aspirin Kenzie had taken eventually kicked in and dulled the pain enough to allow her to enjoy herself. Dinner with the Mullins and Jonah's family was the way she'd always imagined a family dinner should be. Pippa was having the time of her life experiencing what a relaxed meal with good friends could be like.

With her ex-husband's insistence on everything being perfect, from the table setting to the food presentation, their dinner parties had always been subdued affairs that were more about style and networking than friendship. Even when she'd been in the best of health, Kenzie had found entertaining exhausting.

"How are you doing?"

Kenzie jumped at Jonah's voice right next to her. She'd been so absorbed by her thoughts that she'd missed whatever everyone was laughing at. Jonah must have noticed how distracted she was.

Forcing a smile, she said, "Yeah, I'm fine. Just spaced out for a minute."

"You seem to be feeling a bit better." Jonah's return smile was tinged with sadness. "I hope you're having a good time."

"Yes!" Kenzie's emphatic response surprised even her. "It's so great to see Diane and Paul together at last and have such a fun meal. I'm used to dinners being very formal."

His eyebrows quirked up. "You've never had a fun family dinner?"

"Well…" She thought back to meals with her late parents, then with her husband and Pippa. "Both my mother and my ex were perfectionists. You remember Greg Halloran, right? I think you met him a couple of times."

Jonah lifted a shoulder. "He seemed very nice, if a bit tightly wound."

"He could be very exacting, wanting everything to be just so. Which is a great quality in a television producer but can be a bit stressful when it comes to entertaining."

"That's too bad."

Frowning slightly, Kenzie called to mind the last dinner party she and Greg had given. "He has a firmly fixed idea of what things should look like. It was kind of like he wanted to create a set rather than a good time." She gave her head a rueful shake. "Even our family vacations were more about how things looked than how much we enjoyed ourselves." Glancing around the room at the laughing group, she couldn't suppress a huge smile. "He would never have gone for this. Way too laid-back. But Pippa's having a great time."

"And what about you, Kenz?"

His gentle concern created a rush of affection that she quickly stomped on. "Good! I'm good. If Pip's happy, I'm happy."

Was it her imagination, or did Jonah move a bit closer to her? Her knee felt warm where he brushed against it. "She seems very happy here, don't you think?"

"Yes, she does. She adores your family."

Without thinking, Kenzie gave Jonah a sweetly affectionate smile. His eyes widened with surprise, and then he returned the smile and touched her arm gently. "I hope you do, too."

Kenzie's internal alarm went off. Her smile drooped and she jumped to her feet. "I—I should circulate."

With that, Kenzie wandered over to the group gathered around the spinet piano, which Paul played with impressive ease. Jonah saw Pippa run to her mother and drag her closer to the piano. Then the little girl came up to Jonah. "Why aren't you singing, Mr. Raymond?"

"I'm a terrible singer," he admitted. "Everyone is better off if I'm just the audience."

"But—" Pippa hesitated. "But you don't have to be a good

singer. Singing is fun." She glanced back at the group clustered around the piano. "Frankie won't sing either, but I know he likes it when we sing together, when we're playing."

"Sometimes he's shy, especially with a lot of people around."

"But why?" Pippa's face grew more concerned. "How did he get shy?"

Smiling, Jonah took her hands in his. "You don't know what it's like to feel shy, do you?"

She shook her head. "It seems… I don't know, like it doesn't really help anything. But Frankie…" Pippa looked back toward the group, where Frankie stood just outside of the circle, staring at the floor. "It just seems sad."

Jonah noticed Kenzie glancing in their direction, her face worried. Did she not like Pippa talking to him? "Maybe you should go back over there."

But Pippa obviously had something on her mind. "Mr. Raymond, why is Frankie sad?"

Jonah tried not to let his emotion show on his face. "Didn't he tell you why?"

"I mean, a little, but he's so lucky." Pippa sighed. "He has you and Jolie and Miss Diane and Mr. Paul. That's…" She paused to count on her fingers. "That's four whole people, and they're all his family!" Throwing her arms around his neck, Pippa whispered in his ear. "I wish you were my family."

Then she flew over to Frankie without looking back.

Enid slipped next to Jonah on the sofa. "I haven't had a chance to talk to you yet. How are you doing, Jonah?"

"Okay," he said automatically. "How are you?"

Enid shook her head. "Watching your interchange with Kenzie and Pippa just now made me wonder."

Jonah felt himself tense up. "About what?"

"About our talk the other day." She put a gentle hand on his forearm. "I know it must be hard when you work and live so close to each other. Are you sure you're going to be able to keep your distance?"

Jonah gave a vehement nod. "Yes. In fact, we've discussed it and we both agree that there's no way we'd get back together."

Enid pursed her lips. "I don't know, Jonah. From what I saw just now, you still care about her very much."

His throat tightened and he had to clear it to respond. "Okay, maybe I care a bit. I mean, she was the love of my life—"

Enid inhaled audibly. "The love of your life? I'd thought that was Elena."

Frustrated, Jonah studied his hands. "It's a long, complicated story. I wanted to marry Kenzie, but she got mad at me about something and took a job in California. Elena stood by me for years before she convinced me we should get married and adopt Frankie. I did love her, but not the same way I'd loved Kenzie."

Enid started to respond, but Paul's big, hearty voice cut her off.

"Do you little guys know this one?" he asked, his big hands rippling gracefully over the keys to tease out a familiar hymn. "It's about thanking God for blessings."

Pippa nodded. "Mommy thanks God all the time. And she taught me to do it, too."

Paul beamed at Pippa and ruffled her curls. "Good for your mommy for teaching you to pray."

Brows furrowed, Frankie scowled at his uncle. "Praying is dumb."

"Franklin!" Jonah's tone held a warning.

Paul had turned to his nephew with simple curiosity. "Why do you say that, buddy?"

"'Cause it's dumb. It doesn't work."

Diane moved over to the boy. "It works if it brings us closer to God."

To Jonah's surprise, Frankie pulled away from his beloved aunt. "It's dumb."

"Franklin!" This time Jonah's voice was louder, making Kenzie jump as he took hold of Frankie's arm.

Pippa wheeled around and glared up at Jonah. "Don't yell at him!" Her own voice could probably be heard for miles.

It was Kenzie's turn to rush to her child and take her by the arm. "Philippa, don't you ever speak to anyone like that, especially not a grown-up!"

Pippa frowned at her mother. "But he yelled first!" The little girl pulled herself free, went to Frankie and grabbed his hand. "Mommy, can't we 'dopt Frankie? Please? He really wants us to 'cause you're nice and he wants a mommy."

Jonah's grip on Frankie loosened and he knelt down next to the boy. His anger changed to sorrow. "Buddy, do you really not want me to adopt you anymore?"

"Can we, Mommy? Please?" Pippa tugged her mother's sleeve. "You told me I was going to have a little brother or sister soon, but it was a really long time ago now and it never happened. And I love Frankie. Can't he be my little brother?"

"No, baby girl," Kenzie whispered. "Frankie already has a daddy and a little sister."

"But he wants a mommy! His mommy died." Pippa's dark eyes were solemn as an owl's.

Kenzie shook her head and frowned Pippa into silence.

"You're never gonna 'dopt me," Frankie growled at his father.

"Yes, I am." Astonished and grieved by the accusation, Jonah felt as if the bottom had dropped out of his world. "It takes time, buddy."

"They won't let you 'cause Mommy died." The boy dragged his sleeve across his eyes and scowled harder. "And I don't want you to, anyway. I want a mommy."

Enid came up behind Frankie and placed her hands on his shoulders. "Frankie, we all love you. Not just the family you live with, but your whole church family."

Diane knelt in front of the little boy and took his hands in hers. "You know how much we love you, right?"

When his face threatened to crumple, Frankie pulled away. His voice came out tight and tiny. "But you're going to have a baby and then you're not going to love me anymore."

The anguish in his son's voice ripped Jonah's heart in two. He reached out to take the boy in his arms again, but Frankie held himself rigid.

"Of course I will!" Diane insisted in her warmest tone. "There's always enough love for everyone. It doesn't get used up."

"That's right, son," Pastor Mullin agreed. "Love just keeps on growing."

Suddenly Frankie became aware of all the eyes fixed on him. Embarrassed, he raced to the door.

Jonah followed him and seized him in a fierce hug. Then, without another word, he lifted the boy off his feet, walked out the door and carried him down the steps to a little bench.

Jonah sat on the bench holding Frankie close and letting him cry his heart out. Jonah was tempted to bawl along with him. His own heart broke over and over at the memory of his son's words.

How had he not realized the root of Frankie's fear? The boy had assumed Jonah was not going to adopt him since Elena had died, while in reality the paperwork had gotten held up after her death but was still in process.

Closing his eyes and holding Frankie close, he prayed silently to a God he was no longer sure was listening to him.

Lord, this is beyond me. Let me know how to comfort my poor little boy. I'm lost and I need You. Help me to find You again.

Chapter Ten

In late September the countryside burst with flaming golds, reds and oranges. Kenzie had often heard the term "leaf peepers" but had never figured out why people would drive around New England just to look at trees. Now she got it. The colors were intense, and right around the backyard pond they were the most breathtaking, a stunning contrast to the deep green of the nearby Christmas trees.

Kenzie's downhill slide continued. Her energy dropped, the physical pain increased and the headaches returned with a vengeance.

She and Jonah sometimes combined their classes so they could work on the harvest pageant together. Set pieces were constructed and painted, costumes pulled together and made festive, and songs of gratitude rang through the downstairs hallway. The first graders worked on perfecting their dance for the farm animal procession.

It was all coming together beautifully despite her conflicted feelings about Jonah, and Kenzie had to admit there was no way she could have done all this coordination without him.

Toward the end of most school days she fought with all her might to stay focused and engaged with the kids. She must have been succeeding because only Jonah seemed to notice that she was anything other than perfectly healthy, and he'd learned to keep his opinion to himself. If he said anything, Kenzie made a point of just smiling and saying she was fine.

Not only was Kenzie feeling sick again, but she was eaten up with worry. What would happen to Pippa if Kenzie fell apart? In the agreement resulting from their divorce, Kenzie had full custody, and Greg seemed to have little interest in exercising his visitation rights. No doubt he was absorbed with his new wife and their impending offspring.

Kenzie had postponed asking Jonah about her messages for so long that she felt awkward about it. Plus, her exhausted brain couldn't figure out how to start that conversation. But given her health issues, she had to find a way soon to ask if he knew he was Pippa's father.

Although Paul was home from his mission and working at his medical practice in the village, Kenzie didn't want to confide in him. Besides, he and Diane were busy with the farm. Anytime they weren't at their regular jobs, they were finishing up the apple harvest, working in the pumpkin patch or tending to the Christmas trees. So she found another local doctor who listened to her concerns, looked at her blood work and shook his head, clearly puzzled.

"There doesn't appear to be anything wrong. All your tests came back normal, or at least within the normal range."

Kenzie's hope of finding an answer deflated. Dr. Alden's words echoed those of doctors she'd seen in Boston, who had insisted that her symptoms were psychosomatic and had labeled her as a hypochondriac. She wondered if those labels had traveled with her to her new home.

"Well, this pain is real whether the tests show a reason or not. I wish someone could figure out what's wrong with me," she sighed.

"You do have a diagnosis of fibromyalgia and possibly chronic fatigue."

"But all these symptoms came on practically overnight," Kenzie explained. "At the same time that I had a huge rash on my right side that started with some kind of insect bite. Is there any way that the Lyme disease test results could be wrong?"

"You've had several Lyme tests over the past couple of years and they all came back negative. But I'm not an infectious disease specialist and it's an extremely controversial illness." Alden squinted at her chart and pursed his lips. "Your liver enzymes are a bit elevated. Do you take a lot of over-the-counter painkillers? Tylenol, aspirin, ibuprofen?"

Kenzie shook her head. "I tend to have a strong reaction to most medications, so I only take something if I'm in really bad shape."

That made him look at her as if she were some rare species. "Even with the constant pain and headaches?" When she shook her head, he set down the paperwork and pressed his fingers into her neck. "Any swollen glands?"

"I had swollen lymph nodes after that bug bite, but they went away." She shrugged. "Sometimes they feel sore, but not swollen."

The doctor picked up her folder again and tapped his pen thoughtfully against the paperwork. "Given your symptoms and the liver count, you may have had mononucleosis recently." At her surprised reaction he added, "Or a similar virus."

"Would that explain all the headaches?" Kenzie asked, pressing her fingers against her throbbing temples.

He nodded. "It could. How long have you had the current one?"

"About a week." She grimaced. "They usually last at least a few days, but lately it's been longer. And light and sound make them worse, which isn't great when you're teaching young children."

The doctor studied her with growing concern. "Are you willing to try prescription medication?" he asked gently.

"At this point I'm willing to try anything," Kenzie admitted.

Dr. Alden nodded. "Good. We need to break you out of

this cycle. Then we can talk about how to manage your headaches and pain in the future. Does that sound good?" When she agreed, he tapped the keys of his computer. "I'm giving you three prescriptions. One is for the general, all-over pain, one for insomnia, and one is specifically for your headaches, which definitely sound like migraines." The little printer next to his computer whizzed and spit out a few slips of paper, which he signed with a scribble and handed to Kenzie. "Get these filled at the pharmacy in town right away, as soon as you're out of here."

Kenzie felt a pang of trepidation. "How strong are they? Like I said, I'm pretty sensitive even to over-the-counter stuff."

"The painkillers and sleeping pills are moderate, but the migraine meds are pretty strong. But you need something strong to break the cycle." The doctor swiveled his chair around to face her again. "I want you to take a migraine pill as soon as possible."

"Okay. Thanks." Kenzie slid off the examination table.

"You're going to need to take some time off from teaching," the doctor advised her. "You need complete rest and quiet to deal with the persistent headaches and get rid of any lingering virus. Once you've picked up the prescriptions, go straight home, take a migraine pill and go to bed."

Kenzie didn't respond. He didn't need to know that she was on her lunch break and was planning to go back to school for the afternoon. She needed some extra time to pick up the prescriptions first, so she texted Jonah, asking him if he'd mind pulling her second graders into the first grade gym class until she got back. He responded right away with a simple thumbs-up, to her relief.

She hated to ask Jonah for favors. Since that night on the porch and the conversation at the Mullins' dinner party, they'd been walking on eggshells around each other at the house, ridiculously polite and aloof. At school their relationship was strictly professional.

The wait at the pharmacy was even longer than she'd feared, but eventually she had a white bag with three identical bottles of pills. Desperate to stop the headache enough to get through the rest of the school day, Kenzie picked out the bottle with the word *migraine* on the label. She washed a pill down in the car outside the pharmacy before driving to the school as quickly as was legal.

Squinting against the sunlight, Kenzie pulled into the school parking lot. The medicine hadn't worked so far, but it had only been about five minutes. She hurriedly parked the Volvo, ran into the building and headed down the stairs.

When Kenzie poked her head into the spacious gym, she found the two classes playing a game of volleyball. Pippa was in the midst of the action, apparently having a wonderful time, her wild red curls bouncing as she jumped and smacked the ball over the net. Kenzie felt a swell of pride in her gregarious, athletic daughter. *I used to be just like that*, she thought with a twist of sadness.

On the other hand, Frankie hung back and watched everyone else play. Even when Pippa trotted over to him, grabbed his hand and tried to coax him out onto the floor, he shook his head and stepped farther back. With a shrug, Pippa ran off to rejoin the game.

Jonah spotted Kenzie and jogged to the doorway. Kenzie couldn't help but notice how his T-shirt showed off his well-muscled arms and chest. She looked away, trying not to blush.

He stood next to her, panting a little. "Hey! I hope this was okay, but it was the only way I could really keep an eye on everyone. I couldn't work on the animal dance because that would leave the second graders with nothing to do."

"No, it's fine. Thanks." When Kenzie turned to look back

at him, suddenly she felt her brain spin inside her head. She grabbed the doorjamb to steady herself.

"Whoa!" Jonah reached out and grabbed her arm. "You okay? You look awfully pale."

Embarrassed, Kenzie forced a laugh. "Just a bit of a headache, but I'm sure it'll go away soon."

"Another headache?" Jonah's concern was etched onto his face. "You get a lot of those, don't you?"

Kenzie shrugged and tried to look nonchalant, although she was starting to feel very strange. "Probably the change in the weather."

"Have you seen a doctor?" he persisted.

"Yup. Actually, I just saw one," she answered as cheerfully as she could. "He gave me a prescription, so I'll be fine."

Jonah was leaning in close. Uncomfortably close. He seemed to be studying her mouth. "Are you sure you're okay? You're kind of slurring your words."

Kenzie tried to laugh but the room was getting weirdly dark, as if storm clouds were gathering inside the gym. When she tried to look around to see what was causing the darkness, her vision narrowed to a tunnel. There was a loud buzzing in her ears as everything disappeared.

Jonah tried to catch Kenzie before she hit the floor, but only managed to break her fall a little so she didn't land too hard. She appeared to have passed out cold and he had no idea why.

Behind him kids were panicking at the sight of their beloved Mrs. Reid lying on the floor. Jonah himself stared in horror for a few seconds before kneeling next to her.

"Mommy!" Pippa shrieked. Before Jonah could stop her, she'd flung herself at Kenzie and was shaking her.

Jonah gently pulled Pippa away from her mother. "Stay back, sweetie. She just fainted. I'm sure she'll be fine, but she needs breathing room, okay?"

As calmly as he could manage, he checked Kenzie's pulse. It was strong but fast, so it probably wasn't a blood pressure drop that had caused her to faint. Her eyes were opening and she seemed to be surprised to find herself on the floor. "What happened?"

"How are you feeling?"

"Embarrassed. Did I actually faint?" Her voice was breathless but the words were clear, so at least she wasn't slurring anymore.

Jonah turned to reassure the kids and discovered Frankie standing frozen next to him, staring at Kenzie with wide, terrified eyes. He appeared to be paralyzed with fear. Maybe somewhere deep in his memory Kenzie's collapse reminded him of sitting beside his unconscious mother when he was a toddler.

Jonah knelt and took his son's hands in his. "Buddy, it's okay. She just fainted. She's going to be okay."

But Frankie's eyes remained locked on his favorite teacher.

Jonah was torn between keeping his attention on Kenzie and comforting Frankie. Then Pippa put her arms around Frankie and hugged him. "It'll be okay, Frankie. She just fainted. See, she's getting up."

Kenzie was easing herself to a sitting position. "What happened?" she asked again.

"Mommy, you fell over!" Pippa yelped.

Jonah put a hand on Kenzie's arm. "I was going to call an ambulance, but—"

"What?" Kenzie sat up so fast she almost fell back again. "I don't need an ambulance!"

"Maybe I should take you to the ER," Jonah said firmly.

Clearly frustrated, Kenzie huffed and wobbled to her feet. She swayed for a moment before straightening up. "I'm fine. See?"

"Mommy, stop being silly!" Pippa ran to her mother and

shook a finger at her like a scolding grown-up. "I don't want you falling over again. You scared Frankie!"

"Oh, no! I'm sorry." Jonah's throat tightened as he watched Kenzie brace herself, walk over to Frankie and give him a hug. "I'm fine, honest! I just got dizzy for a minute. Probably because I skipped lunch."

"See?" Pippa said. "I told you so. She's fine."

At that moment Dr. Mullin hustled through the gym door looking worried. "I was walking by the stairs and heard an uproar. What's going on?" she demanded in her clear, strong voice.

Kenzie tried to look bright and alert. "Nothing."

"Mrs. Reid fell over!" a few kids volunteered, excited now that they knew she was out of danger.

The headmistress hurried over to Kenzie and studied her face, then turned to Jonah. "Go ahead and tell the kids to change. It's almost time for seventh period."

Jonah clapped his hands and yelled, "Okay, kids, class is over. Get your civvies on, pronto!"

The gym magically cleared of six- and seven-year-olds as they ran for the locker rooms, with the exception of Pippa and Frankie. Pippa looked up at Jonah, solemn with worry. "Mr. Raymond, Frankie won't move," she whispered.

Jonah dropped to his knees again and noted that Frankie was standing frozen in the same place, his thumb jammed into his mouth. He'd started that habit again when Elena died but hadn't done it for a few months. He seemed oblivious of his surroundings.

The headmistress joined the little group. "Is he all right?" she asked softly.

Jonah shook his head. "He shuts down when something frightens him, but he'll be okay in a bit. Diane's not working today, so I'll ask her to come get him." He addressed Frankie. "Would you like Auntie Di to take you home? She can let you watch a show or something. Would that make you feel better, son?"

The little boy blinked and focused on his father, still glassy-eyed, and gave a brief nod. Then he seemed to realize he was still sucking his thumb. Quickly he pulled it out of his mouth and hid his hand behind his back, clearly embarrassed.

As Jonah sent a quick text to his sister, Pippa squeezed Frankie's free hand and whispered loudly enough for the adults to hear, "Don't tell my mommy, but when we first moved into your house, I was scared at night, so I sucked my thumb so I could go to sleep."

"Honest?" Frankie's face relaxed when Pippa nodded.

Jonah was deeply touched at how Pippa reassured his son. He almost felt jealous at how Frankie trusted her and responded to her kindness. No wonder he wanted her to be his sister.

His phone buzzed and he glanced at the words on the screen. "Auntie Diane will be here in a few minutes. Can Pippa go home with him?" He looked at Kenzie, who nodded. "Would you like that, buddy?"

"Yes!"

Jonah felt a whoosh of relief when Frankie almost smiled.

The other kids were crowding each other as they ran from the locker rooms. Tessa Adams stopped when she saw Frankie and Pippa huddled together. She burst into derisive laughter, so loud the other children turned to see what she was laughing at.

"Pippa and Frankie sitting in a tree!" Tessa sang. "Pippa, your boyfriend is a baby who sucks his thumb!"

Furious, Pippa stamped her feet and bellowed at the top of her lungs. "Stop being so mean, Tessa Adams! You're one to talk. I saw you picking your nose in science class last week."

All laughter ceased. All eyes turned to Tessa, who looked mortified but lashed right back. "Liar! No, you didn't. You're just embarrassed because your boyfriend is a baby."

Three firm hand claps resonated through the gym. "That's

quite enough, children!" Dr. Mullin glared down at Tessa and Pippa. "Miss Adams, you know better than to make fun of people. And, Miss Halloran, it's kind of you to defend Frankie, but we don't do that by making someone else feel bad, do we?"

While Tessa looked cowed by the headmistress's reprimand, Pippa stared up at her defiantly. "She's always mean to him. She's a bully."

Kenzie seemed to have recovered from her fainting spell. Her voice was firm as she chastised her daughter. "Pippa, apologize to Tessa."

"But, Mommy—"

"This. Minute."

Pippa crossed her arms and stamped her foot in a way all too familiar to Jonah.

She looked like a miniature version of Kenzie eight years ago, furious with him for reasons he still didn't understand, telling him they were through.

Chapter Eleven

Once she was satisfied that Kenzie's fainting spell didn't warrant a trip to the ER, the headmistress took charge. "You don't have a class next period, so you go ahead and take Mrs. Reid's class," she told Jonah, then turned to Kenzie. "You and I are going to have a talk."

When they entered her comfortable, unpretentious office, Dr. Mullin indicated a small sofa and sat next to Kenzie rather than behind her desk. "I'm sure you need a bit of time to sit and feel better. I've been meaning to schedule a meeting with you, and now's as good a time as any."

Although her headache was gone, Kenzie still felt dizzy and unsteady. The vertigo worsened at Dr. Mullin's words and she felt herself turn paler. What if her job was in danger? "Uh-oh."

"No, no! Absolutely no need to worry. You're doing a fine job, by all accounts. I just wanted to offer you some encouragement." Beaming, the headmistress leaned forward to give Kenzie a reassuring smile. "The kids love you and are very engaged with the pageant project, and from what I can see, you're sneaking in a lot of good lessons while they have fun."

Kenzie breathed a sigh of relief. "Thank you, Dr. Mullin."

"Oh, please. Call me Enid. Everyone else does."

"Okay, well, thank you, Enid," Kenzie amended.

"Just a couple of things." Kenzie grimaced at the headmistress's words, causing her to chuckle kindly. "Not about your teaching, by any means," Enid reassured her. "But I have two concerns. Maybe I'm being nosy, but it's important to me to know you're happy." She paused. "And healthy."

A niggle of worry squirmed in Kenzie's stomach. Even on her worst days she tried so hard to act normal, even peppy. But after the medication and fainting spell, she was feeling especially fatigued, and Enid's piercing brown eyes probably didn't miss a trick.

She should have listened to the doctor and gone straight home to rest. And she shouldn't have taken that medication and gone to school until she knew how it would affect her. But the last thing she wanted was to "sick out" so early in her new career. She would power through somehow.

"I just got dizzy for a moment. I should have had lunch." Kenzie managed a rueful smile.

The headmistress studied Kenzie for a moment. "I can see you're a fighter and I'm sure you can fool most people, but it's clear to me that some days you're really struggling."

Kenzie stiffened her spine and raised her chin. "I'm fine. There's absolutely nothing wrong with me." She noticed she was back to quoting what several Boston doctors had told her, which she had adopted as a mantra despite the fact that she didn't believe it.

"Do you have a condition?" Enid asked, ignoring Kenzie's protest. "I know you put on a very brave face, but to me it seems like you're tolerating a lot of physical pain and fatigue. And sometimes you seem a bit unsteady." She put a gentle hand on Kenzie's arm. "Have you seen a doctor, dear heart?"

"I just saw one!" The admission burst out of her. "He couldn't find anything. Just like all the others." Despite her determination to be unemotional, she could feel frustration bubbling up inside her.

Frowning, Enid moved her hand to Kenzie's knee. "Why don't you take a big breath and tell me all about it?"

"I'm sorry," Kenzie choked out. "It's just—I've already seen every doctor in Boston and none of them could figure out what's wrong with me. All the tests came back normal. They finally gave up, told me it's all in my head and to go see a psychiatrist."

"Doctors don't know everything," Enid murmured. "Some of them sure like to think they do, though."

"You can say that again." Shaking her head, Kenzie thought back to how her illness had started. "The thing is that it happened so suddenly. I'd always been super healthy and athletic. Then boom, I became a total wimp."

"You are most certainly not a wimp!" Enid protested.

"Well, I mean, suddenly I started having these weird pains, felt exhausted most of the time, started getting headaches. I'm positive I was bitten by a tick, but the Lyme tests keep coming back negative, so…" She thumped the sofa arm with her fist, dismayed to realize that she was about to start crying.

"Breathe, baby," the headmistress whispered. "What happened with the doctor you saw today?"

Kenzie blew out a tight breath. "He gave me some medication for the headaches and pain, so hopefully that will help."

"Prayer helps, too." Enid offered Kenzie a tissue from a box on the end table.

"I know. At times I've been in so much pain, all I can do is pray." Her mind drifted back to days in Boston when she'd felt so awful she could hardly move, and the wonder of knowing that God was right there with her. "I…I think sometimes God used my weakness to draw me back to Him. Not that He made me ill, but that He saw how much I needed Him."

Enid nodded, her face full of understanding. "The Lord is close to the brokenhearted. Psalm 34. You should read that when you get home. One of my favorites."

Kenzie dabbed at her eyes and blew her nose. "I strayed for a while," she confessed. "When I was in college I kind of gave up on God. But I'm so glad He never gave up on me."

"He's always with us, child," the headmistress murmured. "We turn our backs on Him at times, but He never turns away from us. All we have to do is listen for His voice."

At the sound of the last bell of the school day, Kenzie glanced at the clock. "I should probably get home." She started to get up but Enid stopped her.

"I said I had a couple of things, didn't I?" Kenzie sat back down as Enid stepped to the door and closed it. "I hate to pry, but I have to ask you about your relationship with Jonah Raymond."

That comment gave Kenzie a jolt. "Relationship?"

Enid sat back down, leaning toward Kenzie and keeping her voice low. "Or whatever you want to call it. Sometimes it seems like there's some kind of, I don't know, tension between the two of you."

Kenzie shook her head vehemently. "No, ma'am. There's nothing between us." When Enid kept looking at her, she amended, "Well, there hasn't been anything for a long time."

Enid chuckled and whispered, "Then why are you blushing?" She leaned back and folded her arms. "Funny. Jonah had the same reaction when I asked him that question."

"You—you asked him?" Kenzie swallowed. "And what did he say?"

"He told me that you'd been a couple years ago, but things had ended when you got a job on the West Coast." She lifted her shoulders. "That's all."

"That's correct," Kenzie said quickly.

"Here's the thing." Enid leaned forward again. "I'm not a big fan of romance in the workplace. I just want to make that clear. It tends to get messy and can be very distracting, especially if things go wrong. And it's not great for the kids."

Now that she'd recovered from the surprise, Kenzie made herself speak without emotion. "It's not a problem. On the very first day, Jonah and I agreed to leave the past in the past.

Things didn't end well, so there's no chance we'll ever want to start seeing each other again."

Enid was nodding her approval. "That's good, then. He said the same thing. I'm certainly glad I don't need to worry about any drama!"

"No, ma'am," Kenzie assured her, then hastened to add, "Although you probably should know he's working with me on the harvest pageant."

Enid clapped her hands like an excited child. "Oh my goodness! I'll need to stop in and see what you've come up with."

Kenzie felt a surge of pride. "We have each class working on a different part of the pageant. We'll add a few after-school rehearsals soon, if that's all right."

"Wonderful! And how is Mr. Raymond helping?"

Kenzie couldn't help grinning at the memory of tall, brawny Jonah leading the tiny first graders in their cute dance. "He's working on the farm animals' procession and overseeing the set pieces. And of course, everyone is helping to paint sets and pull costumes together."

Enid clapped again, clearly delighted. "Oh my word, I'm so excited! We're finally having a performance at our little school, and it sounds marvelous!"

"I hope so!" Kenzie glanced at the clock again. "But I really should get going, if we're done for now."

"Absolutely." Enid stood and opened the door. "Thank you for the talk, Mackenzie. Now you go have yourself some time with that precious little girl of yours."

The minute the final bell rang, Jonah hurried to the headmistress's office to wait for Kenzie. He knew she'd drive herself home unless he took some drastic action, and since Frankie and Pippa had already gone home with Diane, he decided to lie in wait and insist she ride home with him instead of driving herself.

As he stood in the hallway by the closed door, he could hear the rise and fall of voices. It was easy to distinguish Kenzie's quick speech from Enid's more deliberate tones, but he couldn't make out any words. He was tempted to move closer to the door and eavesdrop but decided that would not be right. Instead, he leaned against the wall a few feet away and tried to distract himself by checking for messages on his phone.

It didn't work. Not even the text from his sister saying Jolie was napping and Frankie was happily playing with Pippa could mitigate his worry over Kenzie. Was she all right? She'd been in there with Enid for a long time.

At last the door creaked open and Kenzie came out, spotting him right away. "Oh! What are you doing here?"

Was it his imagination or did she look guilty? What on earth had the two ladies been talking about in there?

Jonah's response came out like a teenage boy asking a girl on a date. "Um…so I thought maybe I should give you a ride home."

He could almost hear her armor clank into place. "That's sweet, but not necessary. My car is here."

"I realize that, but I don't think you should drive after passing out like that."

"That was over an hour ago. I'm fine now." And she headed for the door to the parking lot.

Jonah stayed on her heels and took her gently by the arm before she could open the door. "I'm sorry, but I can't allow you to drive."

She shook her head. "But I'm perfectly—"

Enid's resonant voice cut through Kenzie's retort. "Mackenzie, I'm afraid I'll have to agree with Jonah."

The headmistress stood partway through the door to her office, obviously having heard their argument and come out to see what was going on.

"But, Dr. Mullin—I mean, Enid—" Kenzie started to object.

"There are no buts in this situation," the headmistress said firmly. "You passed out cold an hour ago. There is absolutely no way you should be driving." When Kenzie opened her mouth, Enid cut her off again. "And that's final."

With a stern look, the headmistress went back inside her office and closed the door.

Jonah tried hard not to smirk with triumph. "You heard the boss. Let's go."

They walked out to the parking lot together. As soon as they reached their cars, Kenzie demonstrated where her daughter got her defiant attitude by fishing her keys from her purse. "Thanks for walking me to my car. Now I'll be driving myself home."

Jonah deftly grabbed the keys from her hand and held them aloft. "Oh, no, you don't." She whirled around to face him and would have lost her balance if he hadn't caught her. "See that? You're still not steady on your feet. And besides, I'm the health and safety officer for the school." He couldn't help sounding smug as he reminded her of that fact. "It's my responsibility to see that you don't endanger yourself or others. So I forbid you to get in that car."

Jonah should have known that was the wrong thing to say to Mackenzie Reid. She stepped toward him, eyes sparking. "I am perfectly fine. Ask any doctor in Boston."

The statement gave Jonah pause. "Wait—how many doctors have you seen?"

"A lot!" She delivered her answer as if it were a good thing. "And they know more than a school health and safety officer."

Slowly, Jonah shook his head. "If you've seen that many doctors, and you saw another one today who gave you prescriptions, it sounds to me like maybe you have some serious health issues."

Realizing her mistake, Kenzie scowled. She took a moment to think before continuing her argument. "The doctor today gave me medication. I told you I took it for the first time just before I got back to school. That's why I fainted." Even she seemed to recognize the weakness of her words. Her eyes dropped to the pavement at her feet.

Jonah couldn't help being moved by Kenzie's determination. She was trying so hard to be as strong and feisty as her younger self, to rise above whatever was ailing her. He was still holding on to her arm. Without thinking, he slid his hand down and took her hand. "Kenzie, I'm sorry I was so bossy, but it's absolutely true that I need to look after possibly dangerous situations. That includes students and staff who are sick."

"There's nothing wrong with me," she said in a broken whisper.

"Maybe not, but given that you fainted only an hour ago and you're taking some new medication, I don't think it's wise for you to drive. Do you?" Head still hanging, she didn't answer. "What would happen to Pippa if you got in an accident?"

When she looked up at him, the anguish in her eyes almost undid him. He swallowed hard and took her other hand.

"So please let me drive you home. Please. For me." His voice went husky. "I couldn't stand it if something happened to you."

Whoa, where had that come from? He was supposed to be keeping his distance. Instead, he'd basically told her he still cared about her.

She was staring at him, stunned by his words. At least she'd stopped objecting. With uncharacteristic meekness, she slipped into the passenger seat of his car when he opened the door.

As he carefully pulled out of the parking lot, he chuckled. "I can see where your daughter gets her stubbornness."

When he glanced over at Kenzie, she had a very odd expression on her face. "How do you know she doesn't get it from her father?"

From what Jonah could remember of Greg Halloran, he thought it more likely that Pippa would have inherited a chronic case of fussiness from him. But he could feel frost forming in the air between them, so he backtracked hastily. "Hey, I was kidding. Sorry. I know you've had a rough day. I was just trying to lighten things up, that's all."

After a moment, Kenzie sighed and leaned back in her seat. "It's okay." After a moment she added, "But you should know, I'm not the only one responsible for Pippa's personality."

Chapter Twelve

October's three-day weekend could not come soon enough for Kenzie. Her exhaustion and pain seemed to increase every day, no matter how much rest she got. In the mornings she woke up feeling like she'd gotten no sleep at all, but so far she was still able to keep working and acting normal enough not to arouse suspicion.

Dr. Alden's advice to take time off to recover was simply not an option. She'd had the teaching job for such a short time there was no way she could take sick leave, which at this point would be unpaid. The last thing she needed was to lose the one job she'd managed to land. If she'd had no one except herself to worry about, things might have been different, but she needed security for Pippa. Sometimes that was the only thought that kept her going.

Also, work on the harvest pageant was ramping up. So Kenzie kept going, kept working with Jonah to build up the different parts of the pageant so everyone would be ready when they started full rehearsals after the long weekend.

Friday afternoon was the absolute worst. Kenzie barely managed to keep a cheerful facade as she dismissed her final restless class of first graders, walked to the car with Pippa and headed home.

As soon as they'd pulled past the Holiday Farm sign and rolled to a stop in front of the house, Pippa went whooping out of the car to jump in crispy piles of leaves with Frankie. Kenzie meandered into their apartment and sank onto the sofa, vowing not to move again until absolutely necessary.

She thought about the painkillers in her nightstand. A few times lately when the pain had been extra severe and a sleeping pill didn't help, she'd thought about taking half of one painkiller just to reduce the pain enough for her to get to sleep. But given her sensitivity to medication, Kenzie remained determined to stay away from those pills. She knew they held dangers that outweighed their advantages. Right now she felt optimistic that having some quiet time on the sofa would get her through the rest of the day.

Tomorrow she'd chart out a schedule for the final pageant rehearsals, in time for their performance the last week in October. But until then, she could take advantage of the holiday and get some much-needed rest.

She started to flop back on the sofa, but a jarring spasm seized her spine. The pain was so unexpected and intense she unintentionally cried out, then gripped the edge of the sofa with both hands and took harsh, tight breaths to will it away. After a minute her breathing eased a bit and she tried to move, which made her cry out again.

What on earth was happening now?

The apartment door burst open and Pippa galloped into the room with Frankie. "Mommy! Can Frankie come over and play?"

Desperately masking her agony, Kenzie gave her daughter a gentle smile. "I don't think now's a good time. I need a little rest."

Pippa pouted. "You're always sick. It's boring."

Although her daughter needed correction, Kenzie couldn't even summon enough energy for her *don't cross that line* look. "I don't do it on purpose, Pip," she murmured. "I'd much rather not be boring, believe me. Can you go over to Frankie's to play?"

Pippa consulted Frankie, then turned back to her mother. "Jolie's taking a nap. If we're really, really, really quiet can we play here?"

Kenzie started to shake her head but a spasm in her neck stopped her short. "Ow!"

"Mommy?" Now Pippa was alarmed.

"Sorry, baby girl," Kenzie gasped. "But I can't right now. Play outdoors, okay?"

Frankie peeked out from behind Pippa, a stricken look on his face. "Are you going to die?" he quavered.

The boy seemed terrified. Somehow Kenzie found the energy to give him a reassuring smile, even to laugh a little. "I'm not planning on it. It's just a really bad headache, honest. I need to lie down for a bit. Then I'll be fine."

Keeping the smile on her face, she watched as the children tiptoed out and closed the door with exaggerated care behind them. Then she worked herself incrementally to a half-standing, half-crouching position and inched her way across the floor to the bedroom. Every movement sent her spine and ribs into spasms.

It was unquestionably the worst physical pain she'd been in since this affliction had started a couple of years ago. Combined with the now searing migraine, it was enough to make her think seriously about taking a painkiller.

I'm sorry, Lord, she prayed silently. *Please be with me and help me hold on to You.*

She made it all the way into the cool, dark bedroom, where she carefully eased herself onto the bed. But lying down seemed to make the pain explode. She hadn't thought it could get any worse. Apparently she'd been wrong.

"Help me, God!" she prayed aloud as she groped for the nightstand drawer. Her hand located the bottle of migraine pills. Trying to unscrew the cap was almost too much for her, but she finally managed it. Grasping one of the pills, she bit it in half, dry-swallowed it and flopped back on the bed, waiting for the agony to abate.

As Jonah raised his hand to knock on Kenzie's door, Pippa and Frankie came running in from outdoors, their cheeks flushed from playing in the crisp autumn air.

"My mom's asleep." Pippa folded her arms and frowned as if she were a security guard ten times her size. "She said she needs to rest."

Jonah's smile faded. Pippa had been different to him for the past week or so, as if she no longer liked him. Maybe Frankie had told her more stories about how much he yelled, even though Jonah had been more careful than ever to keep his naturally loud voice gentle and soft.

"Okay. I'll try later." With a puzzled glance at Frankie, Jonah started toward their apartment.

A soft click made him turn back. Kenzie's door opened and she peeked out. She looked better than she had earlier at school, although she was still far too pale and had dark circles under her eyes. Her smile seemed unfocused and she held on to the doorjamb for support.

"Oh! Hi, everyone. I thought I heard voices." Her words were a bit slurred, which probably meant she'd taken the migraine medication.

"I told him to go away," Pippa said with a sigh. "But he didn't leave fast enough."

"Pippa! Why on earth would you say something like that?" Although she was scolding her daughter, she sounded as if she were still half asleep.

"He's mean," the little girl replied. When Frankie poked her and shook his head, she shrugged. "What? He is. You said so."

So Jonah was right. His son was still upset about something. Or everything. It was hard to tell lately.

It seemed to take Kenzie an effort to say, "And you are rude, missy. Go to your room right now. Playtime is over."

With a ferocious pout, Pippa stomped into the apartment and disappeared. Frankie turned on his heel and headed across the hall, slamming the door behind him.

"Well, that should wake Jolie up," Jonah muttered.

"Sorry about Pippa." When Kenzie's eyes met Jonah's, she blushed and looked away.

The little moment made his heart skip a beat and he felt a rush of something he shouldn't be feeling. Hadn't he told both himself and Kenzie that getting close would be a mistake? Hadn't he decided he needed to focus on his children?

Then the headmistress's warning from the week before came back to him and Jonah wondered if that was why Kenzie seemed embarrassed.

"Did Enid talk to you about me, by any chance?" he asked.

Kenzie kept her eyes on the floor. "Yes, she did. The day I fainted, actually. I guess she said something to you, too?"

"Yeah." Jonah found his gaze going to the same spot on the floor, between their feet. He tried to lighten the mood by adding, "That wasn't at all awkward."

Kenzie didn't laugh. "I'm glad we said the same thing, anyway."

"Did we?"

"Yeah, you know…it was all over years ago and there's no way we were ever getting back together." She glanced up. "Right?"

Jonah pushed down a twinge of regret. "Yeah, that's what I said." He cleared his throat and looked at her, so pale and vulnerable, so close he wanted to reach out and take her hand. "Anyway, I stopped by because I thought you'd want to talk about the rehearsal schedule."

Kenzie sagged a bit more against the door frame. "Now's really not a good time. Maybe tomorrow?"

"Okay, sure." Jonah moved a little closer and studied her face worriedly. "You look awfully tired, Kenz."

Her eyes moved back to his and he caught his breath at the sadness in her gaze. For a moment neither of them spoke. Jonah had to fight the urge to take her in his arms and comfort her.

Kenzie broke the silence. "I know. I think there's something really wrong with me." A tear rolled down her cheek. "I don't know what to do. I have to keep going, take care of Pip." Her voice shook. "I can't fall apart."

The lump in Jonah's throat made it impossible to say a word. Suddenly he pulled her close. At first she tensed up. Then she relaxed against his chest and allowed him to comfort her. Tenderness washed through him and he felt his own eyes fill. Clearing his throat, he whispered, "Can't your ex take care of Pippa for a while so you can get some rest?"

Her response was muffled by his sweatshirt. "His wife has to be on bed rest for the remainder of her pregnancy, so he's looking after her." With a sniffle, she added, "He seems to have lost interest in Pippa."

A bolt of anger struck Jonah. "How can he possibly—"

Kenzie stiffened and pulled away from him. "It's a long story," she said hastily. "Anyway, I'd better go have a talk with Pippa and get her fed. And I promise we'll talk about the rehearsal schedule tomorrow, okay?" With that, she went back inside her apartment and closed the door softly behind her.

After staring at the door for a while, Jonah shook himself and headed across the hall. He checked on Jolie, who was happily awake and playing in her crib, chattering away at her stuffies. Then he went to Frankie's room, rapping sharply on the closed door before opening it. "Frankie? Buddy, let's talk."

He found the boy sitting sullenly on his bed with a big sketch pad, surrounded by crayons. "I'm busy."

Jonah sat on the bed. "You can keep drawing, but I think you need to let me know why you think I'm mean."

"That's not what I said," Frankie grumbled. "Pippa said it wrong."

"Okay, then what did you say?" When the little boy hesitated, Jonah put a hand on his arm. "This is important to me, Frank. If I'm acting mean or grouchy or whatever, I need to know so I can do better."

Frankie gave him an evasive shrug. "I was talking about the man in my dream who was yelling at my real mommy."

Jonah shook his head. "But you must have said something about me that made Pippa mad at me."

Frankie went completely still, shoulders hunched, eyes fixed on the drawing he was working on. "I told Pippa I wanted you to marry her mommy so she could be my sister, but you said no."

Jonah gave a startled laugh. "Frankie, I can't just go and marry someone because you want me to."

"Why not?" His son looked up at him with innocent, imploring eyes.

Jonah pulled Frankie onto his lap and kissed the top of his head. "Because grown-ups need time to get to know each other before they make that kind of decision."

The little boy looked baffled. "Why? I know I love Pippa, and I met her when you met Mrs. Reid."

Wishing he could be as honest and innocent as a six-year-old, Jonah heaved a sigh. "It's just different for grown-ups, buddy."

Chapter Thirteen

"Mommy?"

Pippa's voice sounded uncharacteristically cautious, as if she didn't really want to talk about whatever was on her mind. Kenzie roused herself from her semi-nap on the sofa, prepared to give her daughter her full attention. "What is it, baby girl?"

Pippa sat next to her mother and wrapped her arms around her as she looked up with a hopeful expression. "Did you ask Daddy to come visit?"

Kenzie had been dreading this moment. It had been a while since she'd sent Greg the email asking him to come visit Pippa, but his only response had been terse and dismissive. She needed to find the words to explain the situation to her daughter. Her brain felt soggy from the unrelenting exhaustion and pain, but she was going to have to do her best.

At first she simply said, "Yes, I emailed him, but—"

The little girl sat upright. "When's he coming?"

"I'm not sure he can."

Pippa's face fell. "Why not?"

"Don't be sad, sweetie." Kenzie took her daughter onto her lap and kissed the top of her head. "Camilla's been sick."

Kenzie's sweatshirt muffled Pippa's voice. "I don't want Camilla to come. I want to see Daddy."

"Pips, what did I say about being respectful?" she sighed. "I get that you miss him, but—"

Her daughter straightened up, a puzzled look on her face. "I don't understand why he doesn't come see me. I mean, he's my daddy. Doesn't he miss me at all?"

Kenzie tried to think of a way to explain mandatory bed rest to a seven-year-old. "Sometimes when mommies are going to have babies, they need to lie down a lot, to make sure the baby will be okay. When that happens, daddies need to be around to take care of the mommies."

"But he's my daddy, too!" Pippa insisted. "And I'm already here!"

Kenzie took a deep breath. "I know, Pips. But we're doing great, aren't we? Don't you love living here? You have all those new friends, and Frankie right next door…"

"Frankie comes from Boston, too," Pippa announced excitedly. "That's where he used to live before…" She clapped a hand over her mouth. "I'm not s'posed to talk about that."

"Did Frankie ask you to keep a secret?" Worry niggled at Kenzie's stomach.

Pippa's eyes shifted away from her mother's. "He said Mr. Raymond isn't his real daddy. He's his…um, his foster daddy." Her red-blond eyebrows met over her nose in a puzzled arc. "I don't know what that means. Something between a real daddy and a 'dopted daddy, Frankie said."

"I'm sure Mr. Raymond loves him like a real daddy."

"His real mommy and his 'dopted mommy died." Pippa turned her troubled gaze back to Kenzie. "He said they got sick and died. I don't like you being sick, Mommy."

"Oh, sweetie!" The niggle blossomed into alarm. Kenzie pulled her little girl close and kissed her over and over. "I have a little trouble now and then, but it's nothing serious."

Scrubbing her eyes with her sleeve, Pippa asked, "If you get really sick, will Daddy take care of me?"

Kenzie blinked back tears of her own. Her usually ebullient daughter had some serious worries, so even though Kenzie felt uncomfortable making the assurance, she said what she needed to say to console the distressed child. "Of course, baby girl."

But I'm not saying which daddy, she thought to herself, realizing she really should have that conversation with Jonah as soon as possible.

"So can you please ask him to come visit? Maybe he didn't see the message."

"Of course I can ask, but, Pips, I told you Camilla is sick and he needs to stay home and take care of her."

For a moment Pippa scrunched up her face into an expression Kenzie recognized as stubborn and determined. Then she turned her eyes up to her mother again. "Does Daddy still live in our house?"

"Yes, of course." When Pippa looked satisfied with the answer, Kenzie found herself worrying again. "Why do you ask?"

"No reason. Does Camilla live there, too?"

"Of course she does. She and your daddy are married." Kenzie put her hand under Pippa's chin and studied her face, which was an interesting mix of sly and innocent. "Why are you asking so many questions?"

With an elaborate shrug, Pippa answered, "I thought maybe we could go visit him there, if he can't come here."

Kenzie considered Pippa's suggestion, then shook her head. "Maybe after the baby is born," she said cautiously, "but I don't think Camilla needs visitors right now." She tickled Pippa to lighten the moment. "Especially a little girl with a big mouth!"

"I do not!" Pippa yelled at the top of her lungs, squealing and kicking.

Kenzie put her hands over her ears playfully. "I rest my case. That was super loud."

"I can be quiet! And you said Mr. Raymond has a big voice, and sometimes it sounds like he's yelling when he isn't even mad. Maybe I'm like that, too."

Her daughter's words froze Kenzie, who found herself wondering if that was where Pippa got her tendency to shout. She was very familiar with the power of Jonah's voice. With the gym right across the hall from her arts classroom, it was hard to ignore. "It's true. Some people have big voices. But they can learn to tone it down, right?"

"Mommy, I'm trying to be less shouty. I know you and Daddy don't like when I'm loud." Pippa gave her shoulders an exaggerated shrug. "Because if you're shouty all the time, how can people tell when you're mad?"

"You've got a point, baby girl." As she spoke, Kenzie felt exhaustion sweep through her body, intensifying the all-over ache that never seemed to go away. Her automatic reaction was to sit up straighter and breathe deeply.

"Mommy?" Pippa peered at her mother with earnest concern. "Are you hurting again?"

"I'm fine, just a little tired."

Kenzie always did her best to hide her symptoms from Pippa, but it had been getting more and more difficult. At the moment it seemed as if every cell of her body was on fire.

In spite of the growing intensity of her pain, she'd steadily resisted even trying one of the painkillers Dr. Alden had prescribed. Taking pain medication while teaching seemed like a terrible idea. Taking pain medication as the single mother of an active child seemed even worse. But she could treat the impending migraine as long as she took only half a pill.

"I just need to take something for my headache," she explained as she struggled up from the sofa. "Then I'll be fine."

"Okay, Mommy." Pippa glanced through the picture window behind the sofa. A big grin spread across her face and she started waving frantically. "May I please go outside and play with Frankie?"

"Yes, but bundle up first and stay close so I can see you from here." Kenzie managed to gasp out the instructions as she hobbled to her bedroom to get a pill.

Once she'd taken half of a migraine pill, she sat quietly on the sofa, watching the kids play. She was amazed at how well they got on together, considering how different their personalities and backgrounds were. Maybe opposites really did attract. After all, she'd married the serious-minded Greg Halloran and their marriage had been fine until she got sick.

And before that, when she and Jonah were a couple, she'd been the loud one. Pippa could easily have gotten her "shouty-ness" from either parent.

But Frankie certainly could be loud, especially at night. She knew he was still having nightmares that made him wake up screaming.

Because of her persistent pain, Kenzie was having so much trouble sleeping that she either woke up or was already awake when the screaming started. So far Pippa had always slept soundly through the noise—nothing woke that girl up once she was out for the night—but Kenzie found the little boy's pitiful screams so harrowing that she couldn't get back to sleep for hours, if at all.

What had he been through that gave him such horrific nightmares? Despite the fact that her mother and the man she assumed was her father had divorced, Pippa had led a relatively protected childhood. It upset Kenzie deeply to think that a small child like Frankie had witnessed anything that would create such a reaction, but she knew plenty of children were exposed to terrible things.

She burned to help Jonah and Frankie, to find some way to guide them through the darkness. God had sustained her through her own darkest days. Maybe she could find a way to share her story with Jonah.

A soft rap on the door roused Kenzie from her musings. The migraine pill hadn't kicked in yet and she didn't feel equal to getting up, so she called out, "It's open. Come on in!"

She knew it was unlikely that Jonah would drop by unless

Frankie was there, so she wasn't surprised when Diane's head poked around the door. "Are you up for a visit?"

"Sure!" Not wanting Jonah's sister to worry, Kenzie forced brightness into her voice. "Do you want some coffee or tea?"

Settling next to Kenzie on the sofa, Diane studied her face. "No, thanks. You look beat."

"Just recovering from a week of teaching," Kenzie laughed.

With a sympathetic nod, Diane rested a hand on her stomach. "I don't know how you do it. I know how challenging some of those kids can be."

"They're not so bad." Kenzie made a wry face. "Well, most of them, anyway."

"I haven't even given birth to this one yet and I'm completely wiped out." With a violent yawn she added, "And I have a few more months to go!"

"Pregnancy takes a lot out of you," Kenzie agreed, although her own pregnancy fatigue had been nothing compared to the level of exhaustion she'd experienced over the last two years.

"I'd been told that, but of course I thought I'd be different, being a sturdy farm girl." Diane stifled another yawn, then smiled fondly. "I think Paul would be willing to carry it for me, if that were possible. He's over the moon about being a daddy."

The last word reminded Kenzie of the conversation she'd just had with Pippa. "I don't want to be the proverbial nosy neighbor, and I know this is none of my business..." she started.

"Uh-oh," Diane teased.

"No, really, just tell me to butt out, but what's the story with Frankie?" She made a face at her own bluntness. "I mean, Pippa said both his mothers died. His birth mother and Elena."

Instantly Diane's expression turned to worry. "I didn't think he could possibly remember that, since he was so little."

"Today's the first time Pippa mentioned it to me, but I got the impression they've discussed it more than once."

A line formed over Diane's nose. "Did she say anything more?"

Kenzie frowned, trying to remember the conversation. "I think it was just that his real mother and his foster mother got sick and died."

Worry creased Diane's forehead. "Anything else?"

"Not that I can think of. We were talking about my ex. Pippa wanted to know when..." Kenzie paused, remembering that Diane had no idea Jonah was Pippa's real father. "When my ex was going to come visit."

"Is he coming?" When Kenzie shrugged, Diane shook her head. "I'm glad Frankie has Pippa to talk to. He has a tendency to go inward and get quiet when he's upset. His life has been awfully traumatic and Jonah's doing his best, but he really needed a friend."

"Jonah never told me Frankie's whole history, but it sounds horrific."

"Hmm." Diane appeared to be thinking things over, finding a way to justify sharing the story with Kenzie. Finally she nodded. "Well, as Frankie's favorite teacher, you should probably know a bit more about him."

Kenzie felt her headache easing up as the pill worked its magic. Trying not to appear too eager to hear the story, she edged a little closer to Diane on the sofa. "I'd like to hear it, if you think Jonah won't mind."

"It's pretty rough," Diane warned. "When they were partners in the Boston PD, he and Elena got an anonymous call to one of the seedier parts of the city. Someone complaining that a baby had been screaming and crying for hours and it was keeping them awake. Nice, right?" Disgusted, she shook her head. "They broke in and found a two-year-old sitting next to his mom's body." Taking a deep breath, she explained, "The cause of death was an opioid overdose."

"That's awful," Kenzie breathed, her heart aching for the little boy Jonah had taken in.

"Horrible," Diane agreed. "He was collateral damage in the opioid epidemic."

Guilt jabbed her midsection as Kenzie thought of the untouched pills in her end table. Maybe just having them there was too much of a temptation. She should probably get rid of them. "Was she taking them for pain?"

Diane's face took on a sorrowful, sympathetic expression. "Not the kind of pain you mean, but I'd say yes, she was taking them for pain." Diane sighed, shaking her head.

"That's horrible. The poor thing." Kenzie felt herself tearing up with empathy for the lost soul who was in so much emotional pain she self-medicated. "But she kept her little boy with her. That couldn't have been easy."

"She probably shouldn't have, but yes, she held on to Frankie."

No matter what happened, Kenzie couldn't imagine anything that would make her give up Pippa. Then again, she'd never had a drug problem. "That's how Jonah and Elena met him?"

Diane nodded. "Yes, and according to Jonah, it was love at first sight. Elena latched on to the boy and refused to let go. She had friends who worked with the Department of Children and Families and pulled strings so she could foster him."

Slumping back on the sofa, Kenzie blinked. She'd only met Elena a couple of times, but she'd gotten the impression of a very strong-willed person. "So they were a couple when they found Frankie?"

"Nope. Well, not in the traditional sense. They'd been partners and close friends for years. After you broke up with Jonah and moved away, they started hanging out together. A lot." Diane turned to look at Kenzie with a rueful expression. "I'm sorry to bring that up. But Elena was really worried about him after you left, wanted to be sure he was okay. And I think it was a good thing. He…he wasn't in great shape."

"It's okay." Kenzie felt a lump of guilt form in her stomach. "It was stupid and selfish of me to act the way I did."

"We were all really worried about him. He was truly devastated."

"I'm so sorry. I don't know what I was thinking."

"But I'm sure Elena was over the moon when you quit the field." Diane frowned. "I shouldn't talk about her like that. I mean, they had a good marriage. She was a good wife and a great mother to Frankie, and Jonah seemed happy."

"And they had Jolena."

"Yes, but sadly, that's where it started to go downhill." Changing positions to face Kenzie, Diane leaned forward. "The pregnancy was rough on Elena. Not so much physically as emotionally. She was a mess."

"I can identify." Kenzie smiled, remembering her own mood swings when she was carrying Pippa.

"I bet you were a dream compared to Elena. We'd get phone calls from Jonah three, four times a week, just begging for advice." Diane winced and fidgeted her way to a more comfortable position. "They still lived in Boston and he was still working as a policeman, plus my husband was working a million hours a week because of a doctor shortage, so it wasn't easy for us to drive to Boston and see what was going on for ourselves." Rubbing her belly, she added, "Then the birth was a nightmare. Elena and Jolie were both in danger of not making it."

"That must have been terrifying." Kenzie thought gratefully of her own relatively easy childbirth.

"The upshot was, they told Elena she couldn't have another baby, and she went into one heck of a depression." Diane paused as if thinking whether she should share anything else with Kenzie. After a deep breath, she went on. "Then one day while Jonah was working, she went for a drive, leaving the kids home alone."

Kenzie couldn't stifle a gasp. "Oh, no."

"Oh, yes," Diane confirmed grimly. "Jonah got a call at work that she'd been in a bad accident. Blood tests showed she had taken a few painkillers and probably fell asleep at the wheel. She died the next day."

Kenzie closed her eyes, imagining the horror that Jonah had faced alone. "Poor Frankie."

"Yeah. You can't help thinking it's going to take years for him to overcome what he's been through." Diane blinked back sudden tears. "I can't tell you how much I pray for that boy."

"No wonder he gets so angry," Kenzie whispered.

"The minute we heard, Paul and I ran to Boston and told Jonah they were moving in with us, end of story. He couldn't go on being a city cop when he was left alone with two little kids. I knew a new health and safety position was opening up at the school. It was a no-brainer."

Feeling as if she were in a state of shock and her mouth was on autopilot, Kenzie said, "He's so blessed to have you. They're all so fortunate."

"I guess." Diane made a wry face. "But the last thing I'd call any of them is fortunate."

Stunned with all these new and upsetting details about Jonah and Frankie, Kenzie stared straight ahead of herself without saying a word. Finally Diane reached over and patted her knee, then struggled to her feet. "You look exhausted and I've just given you information overload. I'm going to check in with Jonah, let you get some rest."

Kenzie barely registered Diane leaving the apartment and closing the door softly behind her.

Jonah answered the quick tap on his door knowing it was Diane. Paul was at work in the ER, and Kenzie had never gotten into the habit of dropping by unless she knew Pippa was there playing with Frankie and wanted her to come home. He opened the door with a welcoming smile for his sister.

"Hey." His smile faded at Diane's worried face as she slipped under his arm, closing the door behind her. "Are you all right?"

"Me? Yeah, I'm great!" Placing a hand on her baby bump, she gave him a reassuring grin before making her way over to the living area. "But...well, I was just talking to Kenzie."

Although he couldn't stop his heart from leaping at the mention of Kenzie's name, he also couldn't keep from feeling a jolt of worry. "Uh-oh. What did I do now?"

Diane eased herself onto the sofa with a groan and gave a sigh of contentment as she settled into the deep cushions. "Nothing, as far as I know. But Frankie's been talking to Pippa, who in turn talked to her mother."

"And?" Jonah asked when she paused.

Once her brother was seated in the well-worn recliner, she said, "And he's been telling her that both his mommies got sick and died. Did you tell him about his bio mom?"

Jonah sighed heavily. "No, never. But I think he's remembered a bit. He asked if she had yellow hair."

"And did she?"

He nodded. "Her real hair was dark, almost black. She'd dyed it a bright blond color, but she had a couple inches of dark roots. Is that all he said?"

Diane shrugged. "That's all Pippa said to Kenzie. I guess they were talking about asking the ex to visit and somehow that came up."

Jonah closed his eyes and rested his head on the back of the recliner. "Do you think I should sit him down and let him ask whatever he wants? I mean, he has a right to know about his birth mother." He sighed again, shaking his head. "I wish Elena hadn't told him he wasn't ours."

Diane spoke cautiously. "It's unfortunate, but there's no putting that genie back in the bottle. Maybe you could tell him you knew the minute you saw him that you wanted to be his daddy?"

"That would be the truth, at any rate." In spite of his worries, Jonah felt his heart warming. "And the way Elena took to that boy pretty much saved his life."

His sister reached over to touch his arm. "She had a big heart. And she loved you both fiercely."

"I know. She was a lioness, that's for sure." Blinking back a sudden threat of tears, Jonah studied the ceiling. "But Frankie only just started asking questions. Maybe the memories only just started coming back. Or maybe he started thinking more about Elena telling him he was a foster kid." He glanced back at his sister, shaking his head sadly. "Why she decided to tell that to a messed-up five-year-old, I'll never understand."

"Maybe because she was pretty messed up herself at that point," Diane suggested.

"True," Jonah agreed. "But why is he remembering now? She definitely didn't tell him what happened to his mom."

"Maybe he saw something on TV that jogged his memory?"

"You know I do my best to protect him from all of that stuff, but I can't control what another kid might show him. He spends a lot of time with Pippa these days."

"I very much doubt that Pippa would be allowed to show him much of anything," Diane said gently. "From what I've seen, Kenzie is a very vigilant mother. It's probably just a recovered memory. Maybe he blocked it for a while, but now that he knows he's safe and loved, it's coming back."

"I'm not so sure how safe he feels." Jonah sagged back into the recliner. "I know he feels I'm letting him down because the adoption process is dragging on and on. I've tried to explain it, but it gets a bit messy since it's because of Elena's death."

"So he actually thinks you don't want to adopt him?"

Heart aching, Jonah nodded. "Sometimes it's pretty clear that that's what he believes. That's what his meltdown was about at the Mullins' dinner."

"Not surprising," Diane said gently. "He may be afraid of losing you, like he's lost his other parents."

"He says over and over that he wants a mom," Jonah murmured. "In fact, he pretty much ordered me to marry Kenzie so Pippa could be his sister."

Diane's eyes gleamed with mischief. "Yes, he seems very fond of our neighbor." She shot him a playful wink. "And so do you."

Jonah ran his hands through his hair. "Stop it. That ship sailed about eight years ago. And besides, I need to focus on the kids. I told you that."

"Easier to do when you have a helpmate, don't ya think?" When Jonah started to retort, Diane cut him off. "Okay, so you guys had a bad breakup eight years ago. Now you've both had time to grow up and get over it, maybe you could at least try dating each other again and see what happens. What's the problem?"

"The problem is I don't think she likes me very much. Sometimes I think she hates my guts."

"Are you kidding me?" Diane reached over again, this time to punch Jonah's arm. "She's just putting on an act."

"It's one very convincing act."

"Well, you're a clueless guy. I'm female, she's female. I'm on to all those little things we do to pretend we're not madly in love with some guy. And that includes acting like we hate your guts when, in fact, we're seriously crazy about your guts."

Jonah burst out laughing. "Well, that sounds gross."

"It's not gross. It's human nature."

"Di, trust me. Kenzie wants nothing to do with me. She's made it clear again and again."

"That just proves what I'm saying," Diane insisted. "If she didn't care, she wouldn't protest so much."

Jonah was deep in thought. "I wish I knew what I did that made her so mad."

"What? When?"

He shook his head. "Eight years ago, when she just dumped me out of nowhere."

"Did you ask her?"

"I did at the time, but she seemed to think I should know what I'd done."

"Okay." Diane folded her arms across her chest. "Tell me everything."

Jonah turned to her as he thought back. "We'd gone camping the weekend before. It was her first time. She hated it, and I couldn't blame her. The weather turned awful, it was cold and wet, and she was miserable."

"But she didn't dump you then? 'Cause I would've."

He grimaced as he recalled that ill-advised trip. "We had separate tents, but when it started raining hers collapsed. So she came in with me, and…" Jonah could feel his face heating up.

Diane didn't miss a trick. Her mouth dropped open. "Whoa. Okay, this is new information. And it could explain a lot. Then what?"

"As soon as we got back, I dropped Kenzie at her place and took off for Mom's to get Grandma's engagement ring."

Diane's mouth formed an O. "Did Kenzie know what you were up to?"

"Of course not! I stayed a week because Mom needed some stuff done around the house, and…well, I didn't talk to Kenzie much." When Diane gave him a look, Jonah added, "She was getting through her last round of tests and interviewing for jobs, so I didn't want to interrupt her."

Comprehension dawned on Diane's face. "Ah. Now I'm starting to see where you may have messed up, dear brother."

Jonah looked perplexed. "Well, please enlighten me, dear sister."

"Seriously? You really are clueless." Diane counted off his sins on her fingers. "One, you drag the girl off on a camping trip that she hates. Two, you take things to a new level, right?" Jonah nodded. "Three, you take off for a week and hardly ever call."

"Um…well, more or less," Jonah muttered.

"Wow. And all she did was dump you?" Diane burst out laughing. "Do you know anything about women at all?"

Before he could answer, there was a loud, frantic banging on the door. A feeling of foreboding made Jonah leap to his feet and run to open it. When he did, Kenzie collapsed against him as if her legs had given out.

"The kids," she gasped. "They're gone. I can't see them anywhere."

Chapter Fourteen

Even before Kenzie had finished speaking, Jonah and Diane had both run past her into the foyer. Jonah knew the kids sometimes played in a part of the yard that wasn't visible from Kenzie's place, so he ran out the back door. Craning his neck, he peered all around the area near the porch, certain he'd spot Frankie's bright red coat.

Nothing.

As he hurried down the steps to the yard, Diane and Kenzie came panting around the corner. "No sign of them out front," Diane huffed.

"The pond!" Kenzie pointed a shaking finger toward the path leading to the pond before she started her wobbly way down.

Jonah turned to his sister. "You go inside and check all around the house, okay? I'll go to the pond, too." Without waiting for a response, he ran after Kenzie.

Despite her obvious unsteadiness, Kenzie was making her way down the path with that old familiar look of determination. "It's my fault," she choked out, slipping on wet leaves. "I should have been watching."

Jonah took her arm to keep her from falling, then kept holding on to her as they approached the pond's edge. His stomach filled with dread. He'd always been so careful to warn Frankie to keep his distance, but lately the boy's moods had been unpredictable.

Although a stunning landscape for much of the year, the pond was gray and bleak on this overcast day. Brown reeds poked through the dead leaves, which covered the boulders scattered along the edge of the water.

Scanning the expanse for signs of the children, he didn't speak his fears out loud, but his heart sank into his shoes. The pond had boulders sticking out that might look very tempting as stepping stones to a six- and seven-year-old. It would be all too easy to slip and fall into the water, which was very deep in places. He held his breath and kept looking around the little pond, praying harder than he'd ever prayed in his life.

Dear Lord, please keep our children safe. Please have them be hiding somewhere nearby. Please, God, please...

"I don't see any footprints in the mud," Kenzie whispered. "That's good, right?"

Jonah realized he had put his arm around her shoulders in a protective gesture. He gave her a reassuring squeeze as he recognized that she was right. No footprints. No sign that the kids had been here recently. "Yes, that's good."

He felt her sag against him again. "Then where are they?"

Fighting off the surge of fear that threatened to overwhelm him, Jonah guided Kenzie back to the house. He couldn't let her go by herself, given how shaky she was. It seemed as if she could barely hold herself upright, let alone navigate the muddy path without slipping. "Let's see if Diane found them. If not, I'll take a walk around the whole property in case they just wandered somewhere we can't see."

But as Jonah helped Kenzie up the porch steps, Diane appeared at the back door with Jolie in her arms. "They're nowhere in the house. I've been everywhere, calling their names."

Jonah hadn't thought he could feel any more distressed. Somehow he kept his voice calm and authoritative. "Call the police. Now. I'll keep looking around the yard." He went back down the steps and started his search, terrified of what he might find.

Or not find.

"I was sitting on the sofa, watching them through the window. I told them not to leave my sight. But I must have dozed off. When I looked out again they were gone."

Kenzie could hardly recognize the emotion-free words coming from her mouth. She felt like she was a million miles away, listening to some robot drone at the policewoman taking her statement.

"Then you say you looked all around the property, ma'am?" Officer Brooks asked.

"All four of us did, yes."

Kenzie, Diane, Jonah and Paul were gathered around the table in Jonah's eat-in kitchen for the interview. The vibrant yellow walls, the refrigerator covered with Frankie's colorful artwork—the whole atmosphere was at odds with the horror of the situation. In her high chair, Jolie kicked her bootee'd feet and picked at the Cheerios on the tray, cheerfully oblivious to the drama.

"And you two are the kids' parents?" The officer indicated Kenzie and Jonah.

"Yes." Raw with emotion, the single syllable eloquently conveyed Jonah's stress level.

"I'm the little girl's mother, and he's the boy's father," Kenzie explained in that eerie monotone. "We're neighbors."

"Yes, ma'am, I understand that. You didn't see anyone come into the yard?" Studying the officer's elaborately braided hair, Kenzie shook her head. "And you didn't see the kids leave, obviously."

"No."

Brooks leaned forward and tried to catch Kenzie's eyes. "Are you okay, ma'am?"

"Yes, I'm fine, thank you." Actually, she felt numb, as if her entire body had been injected with Novocain. Maybe she shouldn't have taken that migraine pill. It had made her doze off and now the kids were missing and it was all her fault.

Suddenly she became aware that the police officer was asking her a question, her intense brown eyes boring into Kenzie's unfocused ones. "Ma'am, have you been drinking, or have you taken any drugs?"

Jonah exploded. "Are you kidding me? Can we please talk about the missing children?"

Brooks turned to him with a sympathetic look. "Mr. Raymond, you know we have an Amber Alert out and officers are looking throughout the village. We're doing everything we can. The more information we have, the better our chances of finding them." She turned back to Kenzie. "I'm only asking because you seem pretty out of it, to tell the truth. Now, I don't smell alcohol on your breath, but have you taken anything at all? Maybe an antihistamine, something that might make you sleepy?"

"I took part of a migraine pill, but…" Kenzie shook her head, dazed. "I feel really weird."

Paul cut her off. "As a doctor, I'd say she's in shock." He gave her an encouraging squeeze on the shoulder. "She feels terrible for losing sight of the kids. When I got here she was frantic, worried sick. Then she just kinda shut down."

Still peering into Kenzie's face, Brooks shook her head. "She seems like she's ready to fall asleep. And frankly, she doesn't seem all that worried."

When Paul joined the officer in her study of Kenzie, she noticed a flicker of doubt flash through his eyes. But when he straightened up again, he said, "Like I said, she's shut down emotionally, gone into shock. It's a method of coping with extreme stress and grief. So as Jonah says, let's focus on what matters."

Rousing herself to appear more normal, Kenzie mumbled through lips that didn't want to work. "We should be out there looking for them."

But Brooks shook her head again, slow but decisive. "No, ma'am, we need you and Mr. Raymond to stay put, in case the kids come home. You don't want them coming back to an empty house, do you?"

The thought of Pippa coming home and not finding her mother pierced some part of Kenzie's protective layer. A sob escaped her. When Jonah slipped his arm around her shoulders, she fell against him, crying so hard she was shaking.

"I think that's enough for now." Paul made it sound like a suggestion.

"Just one more question, sir." Brooks glanced at Kenzie, struggling to get herself under control, and at Jonah, who kept his arm firmly around her shoulders. "Is there anything the kids said that might indicate where they went? I mean, like maybe they said they wanted candy and decided to walk into the village."

Kenzie dug through the slush of her brain and came up empty. "Pippa knows not to leave the yard, or even play in the front of the house. She knows I need to see her from my window."

"Same goes for Frankie," Jonah agreed. "He knows to stay where we can easily keep an eye on him."

"Boston!" Out of nowhere, Kenzie's brain kicked into gear. "Pippa was just saying this morning she wanted to see her— her father. She asked me if we could go to Boston to see him. And she said something about that being where Frankie used to live." She turned to Jonah. "Do you think…?"

"Boston?" Jonah rubbed his forehead. "How would they get there? They wouldn't hitchhike, would they?"

"We'll check on the main roads leading out of the village, and the bus station downtown." Right away Brooks was on her radio, giving quick instructions to her fellow officers. When she was done, she nodded at the family. "That was good thinking. Thanks, Mrs. Reid."

Kenzie was shaking so hard she could barely stay on her chair. "They couldn't have gotten far without money," she quavered. "Oh, please, God, let them be at the bus station."

As she sat there feeling useless, she squeezed her eyes shut and continued her prayer silently, begging God to find the kids and bring them back safely. *Please, Lord, they're so little. They need Your help to find their way home. I promise I'll never take my eyes off them again if only You'll send them back to us.*

When she looked up, Diane and Paul were gone and Officer Brooks was in the living room, having an incomprehensible, static-filled conversation on her police radio. Jonah was still sitting in the chair next to her, his head bowed over his folded hands. Without realizing she was doing it, Kenzie reached over and took his hands in hers.

They sat that way together, their heads bent over their clasped hands, for several minutes. When Jonah eventually released her hands, she felt a jolt of disappointment. Then he drew her into his arms and whispered, "It's going to be all right."

As he said it, the policewoman's radio crackled in the next room and words muffled by static came out. Brooks acknowledged whatever was said and came into the kitchen.

"Two small children matching the descriptions you gave us were spotted by a clerk at the bus station," she said. "They asked for tickets to Boston, but since they didn't have any money or adults with them, they were turned away."

Kenzie jumped to her feet, ready to sprint into the village. "Where are they now?"

Once again, Brooks gave her head a firm shake and pushed Kenzie back down into her chair. "No one saw them after they tried to get on the bus. The CCTV cameras don't show them leaving the station, so we can assume they're still there." Kenzie tried to get up again, but Brooks held her down with gentle force. "Officers are searching the premises and reviewing what the cameras captured. It's not the best-quality footage and jumps around from location to location, but they are pretty sure they never left the station."

"I'm going there now." Kenzie shook herself free from Brooks and Jonah and headed straight for the door.

The officer followed her, took her arm and guided her right back to the chair. "Best you stay here with your neighbor and wait for the kids at home. I promise I'll keep you informed of every update, and they'll bring the kids straight here as soon as they locate them."

"You mean *if* they locate them!" Kenzie wailed. Now that the numbness and shock had worn off, her emotions had come roaring back, out of control.

"You need to calm down, ma'am. We have a good solid lead now," Brooks reassured her. "It's only a matter of time before we find them, since we know where they wanted to go. I know it sounds impossible, but please try to be patient and stay put. Getting yourself all worked up isn't going to help anyone, is it?"

Jonah drew in a shaky breath and put his arms around Kenzie again. "She's right, Kenz. Just take some deep breaths and keep praying."

"Listen to your boyfriend," Brooks chuckled. "He knows what he's saying. I'll leave you two alone."

After inhaling and exhaling deeply a few times, Kenzie managed to raise an eyebrow and fix Jonah with a wry look. "Boyfriend?"

"Well, once upon a time, anyway." He leaned his forehead against hers. "Honestly, Kenz, I never understood why you broke up with me, although…" He sighed and pulled her closer. "Well, I was having a little talk with Diane before all hell broke loose, and I guess maybe after what happened on that camping trip I should have been better at staying in touch."

"Ya think?" Kenzie sniffled. "But I don't think now's the time to go into it."

"Actually, I think it's the perfect time to go into it," Jonah countered. "We both could use a distraction."

Kenzie tried to smile, but it fell apart and she ended up sobbing on Jonah's shoulder. "Pippa…"

"She'll be all right, and so will Frankie." His voice was firm with conviction.

"You don't know that!"

Jonah drew in a tight breath. "You're right. I don't. But while we were praying I felt something."

She pulled back to look at him, curious and hopeful. "What? What did you feel?"

"I don't know how to describe it." Frowning, he thought it over. "Like a light going on inside me, I guess. I felt… It felt like God telling me it was going to be all right, not to worry." He paused, and as Kenzie watched him, his eyes grew bright with tears and his voice grew husky. "I haven't felt anything like that for ages, to be honest. I went to church with Elena pretty regularly in Boston. She was a devout Christian and brought me back to the faith of my childhood. But I abandoned my faith after Elena died. Now I realize I should have worked harder to keep it."

Kenzie felt her own eyes fill at Jonah's confession. "It's the only thing that's kept me going for the past couple of years, besides my little girl. But…" Her throat constricted as her eyes overflowed. "I don't know what I'd do if something happened to Pippa."

"There's no point in thinking the worst, Kenz." He pulled her close again and kissed her forehead. "Is there?"

After a long silence interrupted only by an occasional crackle from Officer Brooks's radio, Kenzie finally found the courage to ask the question that had been haunting her for eight years. "Why didn't you answer any of my messages?"

"Messages?" Jonah sounded puzzled. "I sent responses right away."

Kenzie leaned back in her chair. "Then why didn't I get them?"

"You did get them. You answered them!" Jonah gave his head a slight shake. "Don't you remember? You'd ask how my mom was doing, I'd ask how your final week was going…"

"Not those messages," Kenzie said gently. "The ones I sent from San Francisco, a month or so later."

Now Jonah appeared completely bewildered. "I never got any messages from you after you left."

"I sent you texts, emails, even a certified letter that I know you got because the receipt came back."

Jonah sat back in his chair and stared at her as if she'd lost her mind. "I never saw a single thing from you once you were gone. I would remember, believe me. And I definitely would have answered."

Realizing her suspicions about Elena might be true but reluctant to say anything, Kenzie forced herself to look confused. "I sent at least a dozen, probably more. Then I waited and waited for you to get back to me. I thought you must have blocked me, which is why I finally sent an actual letter. Which you signed for!"

He'd been shaking his head through her entire speech. "I didn't block you, Kenz. I would never do that. Trust me, I was dying to hear from you, but you'd been so clear that you never wanted to hear from me again." He shook his head. "And I never signed for or even saw a letter either."

"I can't imagine what happened," Kenzie protested. "I definitely sent them to the right addresses. I checked and checked because I couldn't understand why you didn't answer."

Brow furrowed, Jonah thought it over. Then suddenly his face lit up with realization.

"Elena. She hung around my place a lot after you were gone.

I'm sure she could access my phone and email and block you." His expression darkened again. "She might have signed for the letter with my name, then not given it to me."

Kenzie pretended to be surprised. "Would she have done that?"

Jonah nodded, and his face grew gentle. "I'm pretty sure she would and did. She told me she thought it would be a bad idea for me to be in touch with you."

"Why?" Kenzie didn't bother to disguise her anger.

"Because I was a complete mess," Jonah admitted. "And Elena was there to clean it up. She saw me at my worst, as I told you, and she wanted to protect me."

Kenzie scowled. "She had no business blocking me like that."

"It came from a good place, believe me. I know it sounds a bit extreme, but she did it out of love and care. I can't be angry with her for that." He cocked his head at Kenzie, curious. "What did the messages say?"

Kenzie's head was spinning as she thought about how to answer such a loaded question. And now she knew the truth about why he didn't acknowledge Pippa as his child.

He had no idea he was Pippa's father.

But now didn't seem like the best time to tell him such momentous news. Mentally she floundered around, looking for something to tell him instead of the whole truth. She finally settled on part of the truth, for now.

"Um…well, I wanted to come back to Boston," she started, but Officer Brooks burst into the kitchen with a big smile on her face.

"The kids are fine."

Jonah and Kenzie were on their feet right away, asking in unison, "Where are they?"

"They turned up in the cargo hold of a bus on its way to Boston, while it was stopped in Sturbridge. They're on their way home in a police car right now. Should be here in an hour."

"They're okay?" Kenzie asked anxiously.

Brooks chuckled. "A touch of motion sickness, from what I hear, but otherwise they're perfectly fine. Except they might be a little bit scared about what Mom and Dad are going to say when they get here." She raised an eyebrow at the pair in front of her. "As well they should be. This goes beyond being naughty, I think."

But Jonah and Kenzie were in each other's arms again, oblivious to Officer Brooks and her opinions.

"They're okay!" Kenzie gasped.

"Told ya," Jonah whispered.

Chapter Fifteen

Within an hour of their discovery, two filthy, slightly green children with hangdog faces were in danger of being hugged to pieces by their respective parents. For now there were no lectures or scolding or punishment, just joy and gratitude that they were safe.

Jonah couldn't remember the last time he'd felt this happy. Probably well over a year ago. Maybe it was just such a huge relief after all the stress of earlier in the day. Or maybe he was thrilled to have his little boy back. And what was more, Frankie seemed thrilled to be back with Jonah.

After a while Kenzie came up for air and held Pippa at arm's length, trying hard to suppress her smile. "Pee-ew, missy, you really stink!"

Pippa scowled at her partner in crime. "It's Frankie's fault! He barfed on me and it made me barf."

"It's Pippa's fault!" Frankie countered. "She dragged me into that dark, smelly place on the bus and it made me sick."

Now that the parents had let go, Paul started to check the kids over with professional efficiency. "I bet it did," he chuckled. "Inhaling diesel fumes is enough to make anyone barf. How are you feeling now?"

"Gross," Pippa said, wrinkling her nose.

Paul put a big hand on her forehead. "Like you're gonna barf some more?"

She shook her head. "No, just really stinky and dirty and slimy. I want a bath."

"What an awfully good idea," Kenzie said dryly. "We'll get you cleaned up. Then Frankie's daddy and I are going to talk to you about what you did." She turned to Jonah. "Right, Frankie's daddy?"

Jonah grinned, then tried to look stern. "You bet, Pippa's mommy."

After Kenzie and Pippa left, Jonah carried Frankie into the bathroom and ran a tub for him while Diane tucked Jolie into her crib. She poked her head into the bathroom. "All okay in here, big bro?"

Jonah looked up from pouring bubble bath under the faucet as Frankie played with a toy boat. "All good, little sis."

"Well, you know where to find us if anyone starts feeling yucky." Diane gave Frankie a wink, which he tried to return but ended up blinking both his eyes hard. With a laugh, his aunt left to go upstairs and join her husband for dinner.

Jonah gently bathed the little boy, then dried him off and dressed him in clean pajamas. "Are you hungry, buddy?"

Frankie pouted. "No. My head hurts."

"I'm not surprised." Jonah gave him a children's aspirin and some saltines. "You should feel better soon."

Sitting in his recliner and holding his son, Jonah felt a rush of love and sympathy for the little boy. He kissed the top of his head and was rewarded with a trusting snuggle.

"I'm sorry, Daddy," Frankie quavered.

"It's okay now, Frankie. It's okay." He kissed the boy again and whispered, "I love you and I'm so glad to have you back home."

Little arms wrapped around his neck and a warm cheek pressed against his own. "I love you, too."

Tears pricked Jonah's eyes. He hadn't heard those words from Frankie in quite a while, and he'd been sure he would never hear them again. Earlier in the day he'd wondered if he'd ever even see Frankie again, and his heart had been ready to break, although he'd held his despair firmly in check.

And God had been merciful.

Thank You, Lord, he prayed silently. Kenzie's words came back to him, from when they'd prayed together earlier.

"It's the only thing that's kept me going for the past couple of years."

The sense of something lighting up inside of him returned. He knew beyond a shadow of a doubt that God had answered his prayer, even though Jonah had turned his back on his faith after Elena's death. Holding Frankie close, he suddenly realized how much he and his son had in common.

Dear Lord, I'm sorry for running away from You. I should have trusted You all along, no matter how bad things got.

Frankie's timid voice interrupted his prayer. "Daddy?"

"Yes, son?"

"Do you really not know who my real daddy is?"

Although he didn't feel prepared to have this conversation after such an exhausting day, Jonah knew he had to be honest and patient with the little boy who called him "Daddy." Gently he cleared his throat and set Frankie on his knee so they could see each other. "No, son, I really don't."

"Why not? Didn't my real mommy tell you?"

Jonah had to think long and hard about how to answer that question. Finally he decided he didn't need to be literal with an emotionally scarred six-year-old, but he wanted to be technically honest. "No, son, because I never really met your mommy."

Frankie's brows came together over his nose as the boy tried to figure that out. "Then how did you meet me?"

Again, Jonah tried not to be angry with Elena for telling the boy things he was too young to understand. "Mommy Elena and I decided we wanted to adopt a little boy. When we met you, we knew you were the little boy we wanted more than any other."

He had the joy of watching Frankie's face light up, which made telling the shaded truth completely worthwhile. "Honest?"

Grinning back, Jonah nodded. "Honest. We saw you and we knew right away you were supposed to be our little boy."

After a moment Frankie's smile dimmed. "Why did Mommy Elena have to die?"

The boy just couldn't seem to stop throwing the hardest possible questions at him tonight. Jonah tried to think of a reasonable answer, then realized he really could tell the truth this time.

"I don't know."

"But I thought you knew everything!"

"Nope. I don't, and that's the truth." He held Frankie close again and kissed him. "Only God knows everything, son."

Meanwhile Kenzie helped her freshly bathed daughter put on her favorite flannel pajamas, covered with wild horses galloping and rearing. After she'd pulled the top over Pippa's head, she couldn't help throwing her arms around the girl and holding her close. The horror she'd felt at the mere thought of losing Pippa still hadn't worn off.

Pippa often pulled away when her mother was overly demonstrative, but tonight she submitted willingly and even hugged her back. "Are you still sad, Mommy?"

"Not sad at all, sweetie. Just so, so happy you're home safe."

"Are we still going next door?" Pippa asked the question over a huge yawn.

Releasing her daughter and wiping her eyes, Kenzie nodded. "Yes, I think we need to talk all together about what happened. But we'll keep it short so you can go to bed."

Pippa looked up at her mother. "It's okay. I want to be a good girl and do what you tell me."

Kenzie couldn't help laughing. "We'll see how long that lasts."

Together they walked across the softly lit foyer, past the staircase and to Jonah's door. Kenzie tapped lightly. "Jolie is probably sleeping, so let's be very quiet," she whispered to Pippa.

"Come on in!" Jonah's usually boisterous voice was hushed.

She eased the door open to find Jonah sitting in his recliner with Frankie curled up on his lap. She caught her breath at the loving expression on his face as he cuddled the boy, but she managed to speak around the lump in her throat. "Looks like a pajama party."

Pippa bounced up and down on her slippered feet. "Can we have a pajama party, Mommy?" All Kenzie had to do was raise a single eyebrow and the little girl looked at the floor. "Sorry."

"Have a seat." Jonah nodded to the sofa that was kitty-corner to his recliner in front of the fireplace.

Once Kenzie and Pippa were settled on the sofa, Jonah started the interrogation with kindly firmness. "Now it's our turn to ask questions. We both want to hear from you why you ran away like that."

Frankie's eyes grew big with worry. "It was Pippa's idea."

"But you went along with it," Jonah reminded him.

Pippa frowned. "I came inside to talk to Mommy, but she was sleeping on the sofa. I didn't want to bother her. She's always tired on weekends and I think she took one of her headache pills."

Although Pippa's words struck her with guilt, Kenzie raised an eyebrow again. "So it's my fault you decided to run away because I happened to doze off?"

Her daughter mulled over her mother's suggestion, then nodded vigorously. "Yeah, kinda."

Squashing down another wave of guilt, Kenzie shook her head. "Think again, Pips."

The girl thought longer this time. "Okay, no. I made a bad choice."

"And you made me come with you," Frankie told her.

"I didn't make you!" Pippa snapped. "You said you wanted to find your daddy, remember?"

"Pippa!" Kenzie glared her daughter into submission. "I'm pretty sure this wasn't Frankie's idea. Why did you want to go to Boston?"

Pippa's chin started to tremble. She looked down at her hand as her finger traced around one of the horses on her pajamas. "I thought my daddy would be able to find Frankie's daddy. And I wanted to see my daddy and he wouldn't come here."

Refusing to blame Greg's negligence for Pippa's bad decision, Kenzie asked, "Didn't I tell you why he couldn't come?"

"Yes, so I thought if I went to visit him it would be okay." Tears slid down her freckled cheeks. "But the ticket person said we had to pay a whole lot of money to take the bus and we had to have a grown-up with us. So we sneaked into where they put the luggage when the bus driver wasn't looking." Her face crumpled into a comical expression of disgust. "It was so gross! Then Frankie barfed."

Jonah whispered into Frankie's ear. Frankie nodded and shot his friend a contrite look. "I'm sorry I made you sick, Pippa."

"It was my fault for making you go in there," Pippa admitted.

"What about leaving the yard without permission?" Jonah asked sternly. "Walking all the way to the village without saying anything to either of us?" It was clear to Kenzie that he didn't feel angry anymore and the last thing he wanted to do was scold the boy. But they both knew they needed to make sure it never happened again.

"It was naughty," Frankie whispered.

"It was very naughty."

Jonah's loving expression belied the tone of his deep, stern voice. Kenzie's heart twisted in her chest at the sight, so she turned away to look at Pippa. "And you're a whole year older than Frankie, so even if he went along with you, even if he said he wanted to go, were you right to do this?"

Pippa furrowed her eyebrows and stuck her chin out. "No. I was wrong. But I thought maybe my daddy could find Frankie's daddy since they both live in Boston. And I wanted to see my daddy and I didn't want to go alone."

Kenzie forced her eyes not to stray back toward Jonah as her heart ached at Pippa's words. *Baby girl, your daddy's right here.*

Oblivious, Jonah gently turned his son's head to look at him. "Frankie, I know I haven't been doing the best job since Mommy Elena died, but I promise I'll try as hard as I can from now on. And you tell me if something is wrong or you feel unhappy. Okay?"

"Okay, Daddy."

The little boy snuggled against Jonah, closing his eyes tightly.

Jonah caught his breath as if overwhelmed with the sweetness of the moment. He looked over at Kenzie, who could no longer hold back her tears.

"He told me he thought you were going to send him to an orphanage," Pippa whispered. "He said you don't want to 'dopt him anymore."

"I think he knows that's not true now, sweetie," Kenzie murmured.

Pippa nodded and suddenly burst out crying. "I'm sorry, Mommy. I promise I won't do it ever again."

"You'd better not, or I'll lock you in Rapunzel's tower." Kenzie took the girl's face in her hands and covered it with kisses until she giggled helplessly. "Now it's time for bed. Go across the hall and climb into bed, princess. I'll be there in a few minutes."

Pippa kissed her mother, then went shyly over to Jonah and kissed his cheek. "Night, Mr. Raymond."

A shock went through Kenzie. Her daughter was kissing her real father good-night, and she had no idea.

Clearly taken off guard by the kiss, Jonah took a moment to respond. "Night, Pippa."

Pippa leaned over and kissed Frankie. "Night, Frankie. I'm sorry I made you sick and got you in trouble."

"It's okay, Pippa," Frankie said sleepily. "I'm sorry I threw up on you."

Pippa hesitated a moment longer, then said in a rush, "I love you. I wish you were my little brother." Then she hurried off before anyone had a chance to respond.

Frankie slid off his father's lap. "I'm sleepy. I'm going to bed." As if following Pippa's example, he gave Jonah a kiss. "Night, Daddy." Then he cast a shy look at Kenzie.

Swallowing to open her emotion-choked throat, she smiled at him. "Don't I get a kiss, too?"

The little boy flew over to her, wrapped his arms around her neck and kissed her face. "Night, Mrs. Reid." Embarrassed, he ran to his bedroom and closed the door.

As soon as the kids were gone from the room, a rush of exhaustion almost flattened Kenzie. She tried to hide the effort it took to push herself to her feet. "I'd better go tuck Pippa in."

Jonah walked her to the door, where they both stopped and glanced at each other. Then their eyes locked and they each took a step closer.

Jonah echoed her words to Frankie. "Don't I get a kiss, too?"

A parade of conflicting emotions marched through Kenzie's insides before she gave in. Carefully she got up on her toes and offered Jonah her lips.

The kiss was brief, but so tender and full of affection that they clung to each other afterward.

Although she wanted to stay in his arms forever, Kenzie finally forced herself to let go of him. "I'd better get home."

Gazing down at her with heart-stopping affection, he pushed a stray curl from her cheek. "You get some rest. You must be exhausted from all the stress."

"So must you," Kenzie whispered. "Thank you for being with me and keeping me sane." Remembering how much she'd actually lost it while the children were missing, she made a wry face. "Well, mostly."

"You're welcome. You did the same for me, whether you realize it or not." Jonah leaned down and gave her another quick kiss, this time on the cheek. "Get some rest. I'll see you tomorrow."

Chapter Sixteen

Emotionally, Kenzie felt as if she could fly across the foyer to her apartment. Physically, she could barely drag herself the few yards to her door, every step shooting darts of pain up her legs.

Standing inside the doorway, holding herself up by gripping the frame, she prayed for strength. *Dear Lord, please help me keep fighting so I can be a good mother to my child. Nothing in the world matters as much as she does.*

As that thought crossed her mind, reality seemed to strike her across the face.

Today, as a mother she had failed. Miserably. Her little girl had run away from home in search of the man she believed was her father. Worse, Pippa had basically kidnapped a little boy and endangered both him and herself. Worst of all, both children had disappeared while Kenzie was supposed to be watching them.

It struck her like a lightning bolt: If Pippa was the most important thing in Kenzie's world, wouldn't she be better off with people who could take better care of her?

When she thought about it, she had to admit that everything had happened because something was wrong with her. Whether it was a physical illness or a mental condition, something made her an unfit mother. She was beyond fatigued all the time now. She was in constant pain. She had bouts of vertigo that made driving dangerous. To deal with the symptoms, she was on medications that knocked her out.

None of the doctors she'd seen since then could explain how she'd gone from fiercely energetic and athletic to all but crippled with pain and exhaustion. Despite what they told her, she was sure the Lyme tests were wrong.

But no matter what, no matter who was right and who was wrong, it wasn't getting any better. If anything, it was getting worse. And today proved beyond a shadow of a doubt that she was not up to the task of raising a seven-year-old on her own.

Greg had been a decent, if distant, father. And Camilla was a sweet person. Kenzie had no doubt she'd be an amazing mother to the baby she was now carrying. But trying to foist a strong-willed seven-year-old on a new mother would probably not go over very well. Not to mention that Pippa claimed to dislike her stepmother.

All the joy she'd felt from kissing Jonah whooshed out of her, replaced by despair.

Jonah. He was Pippa's real father, but thanks to Elena's interference, he had no idea.

Kenzie had nearly told him this afternoon, but the timing hadn't been right with all the drama around the kids running away. Should she march—well, stagger—over there right now and finish telling him? Would he take Pippa in as part of his family?

It was an awful lot to ask of the single father to a toddler and a troubled little boy, but at least his sister and brother-in-law were right upstairs. They adored Pippa, and she adored them right back.

As she mulled over these sad thoughts, Kenzie limped to the big comfy couch and collapsed. She'd never felt so completely drained in her life. The pain she'd ignored while the children were missing had gone screeching past the bearable mark. Any kind of stress kicked off all kinds of physical symptoms, which was one reason the doctors had decided her issues were psychosomatic. And today had been nothing if not out-of-control stressful.

Ugh, her brain was fried from all the anxiety. Her eyes did not want to stay open and she could feel a migraine starting up at the base of her skull. There was something she needed to do before she headed to the bedroom. She knew she had to do it quickly, before the headache made looking at a screen impossible.

Dragging her phone from the coffee table, Kenzie typed out a hasty text to Greg.

Please come visit as soon as you can. Pippa ran away with the little boy next door and sneaked on a bus to Boston because she wanted to see you. We need to talk. Hope Camilla is well. xo K

Once she'd sent the text, she dragged herself to the bedroom, put on her pajamas and fell into bed, praying that sleep would come quickly for a change.

She lay completely still, too enervated to move a muscle as the migraine roared to full power. She kept staring at the inside of her eyelids as time ticked by, obsessing about the idea of having Pippa live with someone else. The brain fog didn't allow coherent thoughts. All she could do was go around in circles trying to figure out who would be willing to look after her child.

The migraine pills were right there in her nightstand, along with pills for sleeping, which she should take right now, and pills for pain, which she'd staunchly refused to even try.

Kenzie had no idea how much time had passed when she managed to force her eyelids open, gasping at the overwhelming pain coursing through her body. If she'd thought yesterday was as bad as it was going to get, she was wrong. Very, very wrong.

The breath she took to quell a groan sent spasms through her rib cage and made the migraine throb even harder. The pain was so intense it felt as if someone had whacked her in the back of the head with a sledgehammer. A wave of nausea forced her to haul herself upright, which shot burning arrows throughout her body.

Desperate, she told herself she could handle it. All she had to do was wait for the worst of it to pass.

But the pain didn't die down. If anything, it kept growing, until it was so huge it took up all of Kenzie's mental space. She closed her eyes and made herself focus on the one thing she knew was bigger than her pain.

Lord, please help me bear this. I know You're here with me and You can give me the strength to overcome anything. Please, please, please help me!

Finally she managed to grope for the nightstand and open the drawer where she kept her meds. Turning on the light wasn't an option, so she felt around the drawer blindly. Once she found the migraine vial, it took every bit of determination she had to unscrew the childproof cap, especially in the pitch dark, but she finally managed it.

After dry-swallowing one, she waited for relief.

And waited.

The headache gradually lessened but the body pain did not. It was far too much to allow her to sleep. After waiting as long as she could bear, she groped in the drawer again, this time for the sleeping pills. She wrestled the cap off in the dark and took one. It probably wasn't a great idea to take both pills so close together, but it was hours before Pippa would be up. She'd be fine by then.

Eventually she was drowsy enough to try to snatch bits of sleep.

Stabbing agony in her eye jarred her awake. The migraine

was back full force. She reached for another pill. Gradually she relaxed as it made its way into her bloodstream.

With a sigh of gratitude, Kenzie finally drifted into a deep, dreamless sleep.

Around nine the next morning, while he was cleaning up after breakfast, Jonah heard someone rapping persistently on the door. Puzzled, he listened harder. Diane and Paul wouldn't knock like that. Kenzie? Hoping it was her, he opened the door to find little Pippa looking up at him.

"Well, hi there!" he greeted her.

"Good morning, Mr. Raymond." She tried to peer past him, no doubt looking for Frankie.

"He's getting dressed, but he'll be out in a minute. Come on in."

Pippa followed him into the kitchen and looked longingly at a box of cereal he hadn't put away yet. "Can I have some?"

"Of course." He grabbed a clean bowl and filled it with Cheerios and milk. "Haven't you had your breakfast?"

Shoveling cereal into her mouth as if she'd been on the brink of starvation, Pippa shook her head.

"How's your mom doing?"

"She's still sleeping," Pippa explained. "I think I made her really tired."

Jonah chuckled at Pippa's insight but tried to look stern. "I think you probably did. I hope you behave yourself today."

"I will," Pippa promised. "We can't even go outside 'cause it's yucky out. But we can play with my horse farm."

"Why don't you stay over here and watch a movie?" he suggested. "Give your mom a break."

Pippa's eyes looked up at him pleadingly. "But Frankie likes to play with my horse farm, and it's all set up in my room. We'll be extra super quiet."

"Okay, but you'd better check with your mom before you

do anything," Jonah advised. "Make sure she's okay with what you're doing."

"But she's sleeping!" Pippa objected.

"Just wake her up enough to tell her what you're up to," Jonah insisted. "She'll want to know, believe me, especially after yesterday."

Pippa sighed. "Okay, Mr. Raymond."

Frankie appeared, wearing an enormous football jersey that came down to his feet. "I'm ready! I got dressed all by myself!"

"Hey, isn't that my shirt?" Jonah asked.

"Yeah, but can I borrow it? It's cool!"

"You got a shirt on under there, in case you get too warm?" Jonah smiled as the boy lifted the jersey bottom to show jeans and a shirt underneath. "Good boy. Go ahead and play with Pippa, but keep the noise level way down, okay?"

Jonah kept smiling after the two kids were gone, as he set Jolie down in her playpen. He couldn't seem to stop smiling because he couldn't stop thinking about last night's kiss with Kenzie.

A short, sharp yelp interrupted his reverie. Jonah froze in the middle of wiping down Jolie's high chair tray, wondering where it had come from. Maybe a hawk outside? He listened intently for the sound to repeat, but it didn't.

Then a low, mournful keening started up. A child in distress.

His child.

Grabbing Jolie from her playpen, Jonah sprinted out to the foyer. The wailing grew louder, and it was definitely coming from across the hall.

"Frankie!"

Jonah barged through Kenzie's front door with Jolie tucked under his arm like a football. The kids weren't in the main part of the apartment. The distressed wail was coming from the back of the house, where the bedrooms were. He ran through the open door of the closest room to find both kids standing next to the bed, where Kenzie appeared to be fast asleep.

Frankie stood stock-still, gazing at the sleeping woman, the eerie sound issuing from his mouth.

Jonah knelt and put his free arm around his son. "It's okay, buddy. She's just sleeping."

Pippa turned to him with huge, terrified eyes. "No, Mr. Raymond! I can't wake her up!"

Trying not to show his worry at the situation, Jonah set Jolie on the floor and walked to the bed where Kenzie lay, apparently unconscious. He breathed a sigh of relief when he felt her warm skin and heard her breathing.

"Kenzie?" He shook her gently at first, then a little harder. "Kenzie, wake up!"

"Mommy!" Pippa sobbed. "Mommy, please wake up!"

"Kenzie, it's Jonah. Can you hear me?"

No response at all. Frantic but trying to remain outwardly calm for the children's sake, he glanced around the room for an answer. His gaze landed on the nightstand, its drawer open and showing three vials of prescription medication. He picked them up and scanned the labels. He knew Kenzie took pills for her migraines and sometimes for insomnia, but the third vial stopped his heart.

An opioid for pain. The same medication Frankie's mother had overdosed on. The same medication that Elena had used after her difficult birth, that the medical examiner had found in her bloodstream after her fatal accident.

Not Kenzie. Not her, too. *Please, God, no!*

Forcing himself to act, he pulled out his phone and hit 911, giving terse responses to the operator's questions. Then he texted his sister and her doctor husband to come downstairs ASAP.

"Mommy?" Pippa's voice quavered behind him.

Jonah turned to look at the frightened children, then held

his arms out to them. They both ran to him, burying their faces in his shoulder. When he found his voice again, it came out surprisingly calm. "She'll be okay."

Jonah couldn't keep up with his own racing thoughts. How could Kenzie have been so careless? How much medication had she taken?

The sound of heavy footsteps on the hallway stairs meant that Diane and Paul had gotten his text. Diane took one look at the scene and gathered all three children, shepherding them into the next room.

Paul rushed to the bed and checked Kenzie. "Her heart rate and breathing are a bit slow. You called 911?"

Jonah nodded, then wordlessly indicated the pill bottles on the nightstand.

Paul examined the labels. "Migraine meds, insomnia meds… and an opioid?" Worried, he opened the last vial and peered into it. "It doesn't look like she's taken very many at all, so I'm sure it's not an overdose."

Jonah released a breath he hadn't realized he was holding. "Then what happened?"

At that moment the ambulance pulled into the drive and two uniformed EMTs burst into the house. Paul and Jonah moved away to let them check on Kenzie, Jonah pacing anxiously as he stared at the bed.

This couldn't be happening. It couldn't. Paul said she hadn't overdosed based on the number of pills in the bottle, but what if she had another bottle somewhere? And how long had she been taking opioids, anyway? Didn't she know how dangerous they were?

And Frankie. No matter what had happened, Frankie could not deal with the death of another person he loved. Jonah would not let that happen ever again, no matter how he felt about Kenzie.

He realized his thoughts and emotions were spiraling out of

control, but he couldn't seem to reel them back. Fury, heartbreak, confusion all warred for dominance.

Striding into the living room, Jonah grabbed Frankie in his arms and held him close. "It's okay, Frankie. She's going to be okay." The boy was shaking so hard he could barely stand. His breath came in quick, gulping gasps. "Hush, son. Take a big, slow breath. It's okay."

Frankie wrapped his arms around Jonah's neck in a stranglehold. "Mommy," he sobbed.

Jonah didn't think his heart could break any more, but Frankie's anguished voice proved him wrong. "I know, son," he whispered. "I know. It'll be all right. I promise."

To himself he added, *I'll make sure of it.*

Chapter Seventeen

As she was gradually jarred to consciousness by a strange bumping sensation, Kenzie dragged open her leaden eyelids. She vaguely registered that she was strapped to some kind of platform inside what appeared to be a van packed with technical-looking equipment.

She couldn't move enough to look around and see if anyone was with her. When she tried to talk, she realized there was something covering her mouth and nose.

So she screamed.

"Well, I guess she's awake now," a dry female voice quipped.

"Hey, hey, Kenzie, it's okay." The male voice was familiar, soothing.

Had someone she knew abducted her? Why on earth would anyone do that?

A big hand appeared in front of her eyes and removed the thing that was covering her mouth. "You're in an ambulance on the way to the ER," the familiar voice said. "We found you unconscious in your bed, so we need to check you out."

This surprising information made Kenzie choke. The ensuing panic had her struggling for breath until the big hand slipped the mask back onto her face. "Breathe."

"Pippa?" she gasped.

Paul's big, bearded face came into view with a reassuring smile. "She's fine. Diane's taking care of her. And I just texted to let them know you're awake now, so she won't be worrying." His trademark, beaming smile expanded. "I decided to come along for the ride. Being a doctor has its privileges."

Kenzie craned her neck to look around. She spotted an EMT sitting on the other side of her gurney. "What happened?"

The ambulance came to a stop. "We'll fill you in soon," Paul promised. "Right now we've got to get you inside and settled. Then we'll order you a whole bunch of fun tests and try to figure out what's going on." He rose as the ambulance doors whooshed open and the EMTs deftly whisked her into the hospital.

As soon as she was settled in the ER and hooked up to an IV with something to get rid of her headache and nausea, Paul stood next to her bed and checked her vitals. "How many did you take?"

"How many what?" Kenzie couldn't imagine what he was referring to. Her memories of the preceding night were foggy at best and intertwined with disturbing dreams so vivid they seemed real. She needed time to sort through the mess in her head.

Paul gave her a sympathetic look. "There were several prescription drug bottles in your nightstand. One for migraine medication, one for insomnia and one for painkillers. We need to know how many you took from each vial."

Kenzie thought it over and shook her head, which felt as if it were stuffed with feathers. "I remember I took one migraine pill, then a sleeping pill." Her frown deepened as she strained to remember. "I think I took another migraine pill later on. Or maybe it was a sleeping pill. But I've never taken any of the painkillers."

Paul looked relieved. "That's good. I know Jonah will be glad to hear that."

The fog had cleared enough for Kenzie to realize the mistake she must have made. "I'm very sensitive to medication. I should never have taken a second sleeping pill, especially on top of migraine medication."

His face grew concerned. "Why do you keep them next to your bed, rather than in the medicine cabinet?"

"Because of Pippa. She can be very curious, not to say nosy." Kenzie's feeling of dismay increased as she thought about what Paul had said. "She found me? My poor girl!"

Paul's forehead creased. "So you usually just take one sleeping pill?"

"Not very often, but lately…" Sensing his concern, Kenzie blinked back tears. "I was so exhausted last night I could hardly think straight, but I couldn't get to sleep because of that terrible migraine. I honestly thought the meds would wear off well before Pippa got up."

Jotting notes on a yellow legal pad, Paul nodded solemnly. "So you think you took two migraine pills and one sleeping pill?"

Kenzie nodded. "Pretty sure."

"Anything else?"

"I…I don't think so." Her voice came out small. "My brain is so foggy." Suddenly her eyes flooded with tears. "I can't believe I did that. I must have been way out of it."

"Given the day you had yesterday, it's not surprising." Paul blinked down at his notes, then looked back at Kenzie. "I noticed that all the meds, including the painkillers, were prescribed by Dr. Alden not that long ago. What did he prescribe the opioids for?"

"Because I'm in so much pain all the time!" The admission burst out of her. "It's been going on for over two years now, and no one can tell me what's wrong! All they can say is migraines and fibromyalgia, but not one single doctor can tell me why they came on so suddenly, out of nowhere, and won't go away. They just call me a hypochondriac and tell me to see a psychiatrist."

"Wait—did you say over two years?" Paul's eyes widened with surprise.

Wiping her eyes fiercely, Kenzie nodded. "Dr. Alden thought the pills might help me cope with the pain, but when I looked them up online after I got them, I realized what they are and decided to put them aside. Like I said, I'm hypersensitive to even over-the-counter stuff." She couldn't suppress an ironic smile as she remembered her former, healthy self. "A single aspirin used to knock me out for hours."

Paul raised his shaggy eyebrows. "Wow."

"I can only take half of one of the migraine meds at a time. Otherwise I'm out of it for too long, and I can't do that with Pippa to look after. But I took a whole one last night."

"And the insomnia?"

Kenzie nodded and shrugged. "I only take that when I know I'm not going to get to sleep. Like last night. But I've never taken two of either drug in one night."

Paul sat down in a chair next to the bed and leaned in to listen. "You said this all came on suddenly a couple of years ago."

"It was like someone had just flipped a switch on my health." Even though she hadn't wanted to see a doctor she knew personally, it was a relief to Kenzie to talk to someone who knew her about what she'd been battling. "It was a few weeks after we moved back to Boston." Given how the Boston doctors had reacted when she told them about the bug bite and rash, she hesitated to say anything to Paul. Would he just call her crazy, too?

Briefly taking his eyes from her face, Paul jotted another note onto his pad. "How'd it start? Do you remember the first signs or symptoms?"

"Vividly!" She felt more awake now, as the fog slowly lifted from her brain. "I hardly ever used to get sick, aside from the occasional cold. But one day I woke up with a high fever and terrible headache. I felt sore all over. It was like the flu, except it didn't go away."

Nodding, Paul made another quick note. "Any other symptoms? Swollen glands, maybe?"

Kenzie frowned. "The doctor said I had swollen lymph nodes. Plus, I was so tired I literally couldn't stay awake. They tested me for all kinds of stuff, like MS, lupus, rheumatoid arthritis. Everything came back negative, so they decided I'm a hypochondriac."

Biting his upper lip so his thick mustache flared out, Paul drummed the eraser end of his pencil against the notepad. "Did you ever notice a bug bite or a rash?"

Hope fizzed through Kenzie's veins. Maybe Paul would believe her. "Yes! We spent a week on Martha's Vineyard before going to Boston. I thought I had a spider bite."

"What about Lyme disease? Did they ever test you for that?"

Kenzie was nearly breathless with hope. "A few times, but the test always came back negative."

"False negatives are unfortunately pretty common with Lyme. The routine tests are notoriously unreliable." Paul studied her thoughtfully. "Martha's Vineyard is a Lyme hot spot. One of the worst in the country. What time of year were you there?"

"We'd rented a cottage for the month of July." Her hope grew. "I set my chair near a patch of long grass while Pippa played on the beach."

Paul huffed out a triumphant breath. "We'll get you tested properly as soon as possible. I'll order a Lyme panel and a PET scan to look at your brain."

"My brain?" Kenzie felt a jolt of dismay. "Something might be wrong with my brain?"

Paul made soothing motions with his hands. "If it's been this long you may have some inflammation, but treatment will help. That would explain the worsening migraine attacks. It'll take a while to get all the results, but my gut says we should start antibiotic treatment right away."

"Should I stop taking any of the meds Dr. Alden prescribed?" Kenzie felt anxious at the idea of giving up her migraine medication since she was still getting those headaches so often. She was relieved when Paul shook his head.

"No, those are fine for treating the symptoms, for now. Just pace yourself better, maybe put them somewhere other than right beside your bed so you have to get up if you need them. It'll make you more aware of how much you're taking." He sprang up from the chair and gave Kenzie a cheerful nod. "The antibiotics should get you back to your old self, but it may take time."

As Paul bounced out the door, Kenzie felt her heart flood with optimism.

Maybe she finally had a diagnosis, which meant she could get the treatment she needed.

Maybe all the pain and exhaustion would be history soon, and she'd be a better mother to Pippa.

And maybe, in spite of the misgivings she'd let in last night, she and Jonah really had a second chance.

From the quiet of his apartment, with Frankie napping and Jolie upstairs with her aunt, Jonah heard the slamming of car doors when Paul and Kenzie came home from the ER later that day. He heard Pippa's joyful squeak as she thundered down the stairs from Diane's place and ran outside to throw herself at her mother. And when the front door opened, he could hear Kenzie's loving reassurances that she was fine, that the doctors were going to make her all better.

He knew she was lying to reassure Pippa. Whatever was wrong with her, whatever had been so awful that a doctor had given her a potentially dangerous medication to deal with it, could not have been cured by a few hours in the ER.

There was a sharp knock on his door. Praying it wasn't Kenzie, he rushed to open it and put a finger to his lips when he saw his boisterous brother-in-law standing there.

"Frankie's just fallen asleep," Jonah whispered.

"Oops!" Paul clapped a hand over his mouth as he entered. "Sorry about that."

"Jolie's upstairs with Diane. She wanted to give me and Frankie some quiet time together so I could get him calmed down." Jonah indicated the sofa and sagged back onto his recliner. "He'd been having a pretty rough time, but I finally convinced him to lie down, and he fell asleep right away."

Paul was nodding his big head solemnly. "Seeing Kenzie like that had to be a shock, for both of you."

Jonah blew out a tense breath. "That's an understatement."

There was an awkward silence before Paul asked, "Do you want to know how she is?"

"She sounded fine when she came in just now." Jonah's tone was pure ice. When he wasn't soothing a distraught Frankie, he'd spent the last few hours teaching himself to distrust Mackenzie Reid again. The first time she'd broken his heart he'd pined himself sick. Not this time. He couldn't forgive her for making another rash choice, especially given how it affected his son.

"Dude." Paul sounded shocked at Jonah's attitude. "Seriously, she didn't do anything wrong. She made an honest mistake."

But Jonah was already shaking his head before Paul finished speaking. "I'm not putting Frankie through that again. If we have to move out of here, we will, but I don't want him around her anymore."

Scooting to the edge of the sofa, Paul reached a hand to Jonah's arm. "Okay. I get that you're in protective mode. And it makes absolute sense, on the surface."

"The surface is all a traumatized six-year-old can see," Jonah snapped. He closed his eyes and prayed for calm, then opened them to see Paul's worried face. "Sorry, bud. I'm kinda torn up from being with Frankie the past few hours. You have no idea. He was basically catatonic when I got him out of there."

"But—"

"But nothing. My mind is made up." Jonah furrowed his brow to hide the threat of tears. "We can't deal with another death caused by drugs."

"She's not—"

"No, Paul." Jonah's voice was husky with emotion. "No matter what the reason is for Kenzie to have those pills, I absolutely can't take that risk. I need to put Frankie first. It's what Elena would have wanted if she'd been in her right mind."

After a moment, Paul stood and gave Jonah's shoulder a squeeze. "I think you're being unfair to Kenzie and to yourself, but I get where it's coming from. You're doing it out of love for your boy, and there's no better reason in the world. But trust me when I say you're leaping to conclusions. We can talk about it later, when you're less fried. Now maybe you should get some rest yourself."

Paul tiptoed to the door and closed it quietly behind him, leaving Jonah alone with his thoughts once again.

Was he being unfair? Had Kenzie just made a mistake?

Did it matter? She was taking the same kind of drug that had killed Frankie's birth mother and was responsible for his foster mother's fatal accident.

Another knock on the door interrupted his growing head of steam. This one was quiet and polite. Probably his sister, worried after Paul reported back to her, eager to tell him he'd gotten it all wrong and shouldn't judge Kenzie so harshly.

With a grunt Jonah pushed himself out of the recliner and strode to the door, ready to tell Diane to mind her own business.

But when he flung open the door, it wasn't Diane standing on the threshold with a big happy smile.

It was Kenzie.

Chapter Eighteen

When Kenzie moved forward to enter Jonah's apartment, he took a step back and started to close the door, as if to keep her out. Baffled, Kenzie held on to the door and looked Jonah in the eyes. "What's going on?" she demanded.

His face was a thundercloud as he tried to wrestle the door closed. When Kenzie stuck her foot in the crack, Jonah flung the door open, nudged her out into the foyer and stepped outside, closing the door behind him.

"Frankie's asleep," he informed her in a fierce whisper.

She stared up at him, desperately trying to figure out what had changed since last night. Had she done something she didn't remember while she thought she'd been sleeping? Or was this just Jonah's way, turning his back on her after an emotional encounter?

Whatever it was, Kenzie wasn't having it.

"Excuse me," she stage-whispered back. "I thought maybe you'd want to know how I'm doing."

"I know how you're doing." Icicles hung from Jonah's words. "You're fine."

Stung, furious, Kenzie fought down the tide of hurt that surged in her throat. "Would you at least mind telling me what happened? Why are you suddenly so mad at me?"

He snorted. "Do I really have to tell you?"

"Yes, you do!" She could hardly believe this was the same

man who'd been so tender to her last night. "I honestly have no idea what I did. I think you owe me an explanation, at least."

"You think I owe you an explanation, do you?" Jonah's outrage was palpable. "You think I owe you an explanation after my kid finds you unconscious next to a nightstand full of pills?"

His words were a punch in the stomach. Her hand flew up to her mouth as she realized how that must have looked. She moved her eyes back to Jonah's furious face but she couldn't get any words to come out.

"You never told me you were taking anything like that," he went on. "Do you know what happened to my family last year?"

"It's not what you think." Kenzie's voice was tremulous, breathy. "Jonah. I'm so—"

Jonah cut her off. "Don't bother apologizing. I don't want to hear it. I'm done." He took a sharp breath and added in a strangled voice, "And I don't ever want Frankie to see you or Pippa again."

"Why?"

The child's forlorn cry came from behind Kenzie. She turned to see her distressed little girl staring at her and Jonah, bewildered by his angry ultimatum.

At the same time, Frankie opened the door behind Jonah and glared up at his father. "Why are you being mean to my Pippa, Daddy?"

Kenzie pulled herself together for Pippa's sake, summoning righteous indignation to cover her hurt. "Yes, Mr. Raymond, why don't you explain to the children why they can't play together anymore?"

She watched Jonah tamp down his fury with a deep breath, staring at the floor as he fished for an excuse the children would understand. Finally he glanced at Pippa and spoke somewhat sheepishly. "You talked Frankie into running away."

Frankie tugged at Jonah's arm. "No, Daddy, she didn't. We decided to do it together."

"Well…" Pippa looked ashamed but spoke right up. "Frankie, I think I said it first." She glared up at Jonah. "It was a dumb thing to do, but I already said sorry like a million times."

Frankie pushed past his father and took Pippa's hand. "I love Pippa. She's like my big sister. I want to stay friends with her forever. Please, Daddy?"

Kenzie's heart melted at the sight of their innocent affection, but she knew it was up to Jonah. He still had no idea that he was Pippa's father, and under the current circumstances it seemed best to keep him in the dark.

She wiped her eyes and looked at him, fighting to keep her voice neutral and calm. "We'll abide by your decision, Mr. Raymond. It's your call."

The two children gazed up at him with big, pleading eyes. Kenzie had no idea how he could look at them and not relent on the spot. He was staring at the floor again, hiding his expression, and the silence grew unbearably long.

The sound of car tires in the driveway broke the moment. As far as Kenzie knew, everyone who lived in the house was home. Puzzled, she looked toward the front door as it opened and a very familiar man stepped inside.

She heard Pippa gasp. "Daddy!" she shrieked, flinging herself at the intruder.

"Hello, Philippa." Greg Halloran's voice was calm and cool, as if he were greeting a business acquaintance. Kenzie was instantly reminded of his standoffish attitude toward the little girl, despite her unquestioning adoration.

After all, he was the only father she'd ever known.

Frankie was staring in wonder at the stranger. Jonah hissed, "Frankie, let's go inside," but the little boy was too fascinated by Pippa's father to hear him.

Greg turned to Kenzie and nodded. "How are you doing, Mackenzie?" He peered at her through his wire-framed glasses and frowned. "You're still looking a bit peaked. I thought country living might improve your health."

"It's been a weird day," Kenzie answered dryly. "And that's an understatement. I had no idea you were coming."

He gave her a slow, owlish blink. "I answered your text last night. Didn't you see it?"

"Ah, well." Kenzie attempted to laugh. "I was separated from my phone for a while this morning."

Pippa tugged at Greg's sleeve to get his attention. "Mommy went away in an ambulance! She only just came home."

"An ambulance?" Greg's eyes snapped back to Kenzie. "What happened?"

"It's fine. I'm fine," she assured him. "Just the same old same old, but they might have finally figured out what's wrong with me."

"Well, that's good, I guess." He glanced back down at Pippa as she grabbed Frankie and dragged him over to Greg. "And who might this be?"

"This is my best friend in the whole wide world!" Pippa shot Jonah a triumphant look. "His name is Frankie."

"Is this the little boy you ran away with?" Greg asked. Frankie nodded, embarrassed. "I trust you won't be doing anything that foolish again."

"Of course not, Daddy. Mommy made me promise."

"Me too," Frankie chimed in.

"And that's Frankie's daddy, Mr. Raymond." Pippa pointed at Jonah. "He's being mean right now but he's usually nice."

Kenzie's heart stopped as Greg took a step toward Jonah, hand extended. Would Greg remember Jonah? He'd only met him briefly, a decade ago.

"Glad to meet you, Mr. Raymond." As he shook Jonah's hand, Greg peered at him curiously and Kenzie braced herself. "Wait—I know you. Mr. Raymond. Jonah Raymond?"

"Yes, we met briefly before—"

Greg smiled grimly. "About ten years ago, before you stole my girlfriend." He shot a mock-accusing glance toward Kenzie.

Jonah grimaced. "Well…"

With an affable nod, Greg looked back up at Jonah. "No worries. Water under the bridge. But I do have to ask…"

Greg turned his gaze to Kenzie, who was trying very hard not to sink into the floor. She knew beyond a shadow of a doubt what was coming next. "Greg, maybe not now, okay?" she pleaded.

He talked right over her, reminding Kenzie of far too many moments in their marriage. "Why didn't you tell me you were back with him?"

Through gritted teeth Kenzie managed to say, "I'm not."

"It most certainly looks like you are." Greg studied Jonah through his glasses, then looked back at Kenzie. "Which begs the question, do I need to keep paying child support? We're not exactly rolling in money since I'm paying you alimony and child support. Cami can't work anymore, and with our own baby coming, it's not fair for us to keep paying for your child."

Kenzie had been holding her breath throughout Greg's speech, until she'd gone lightheaded. She tried to flash a message using just her eyes, but Greg continued, oblivious to Kenzie's distress signals. He'd worked himself up into a state of indignation and she knew there was no stopping him. Nevertheless, she gripped the staircase railing to keep from falling over as Greg pointed at Jonah and dropped the bomb.

"What do you want with my money when you've got her real father right here?"

Jonah felt as if he'd been launched into an alternate reality. What was happening? Had Kenzie's ex-husband just accused him of being Pippa's father?

Through his dazed state, Jonah located Kenzie's stunned

face. She was staring at him, gripping the banister as if it were a lifeline, her eyes wide with dismay.

Greg still stood in front of her, clearly not understanding the impact of what he'd said. His eyes darted from Kenzie to Jonah and back again. "What? Don't tell me he didn't know. You said you'd tried everything to reach him back then."

Baffled by all the adult weirdness, Pippa spread her arms out and raised her shoulders in an exaggerated shrug and exclaimed, "What's going on? What are you guys talking about?"

To Jonah's relief, Frankie looked completely lost. Neither child seemed to have grasped what Greg had said. Jonah could hardly grasp it himself.

He was Pippa's father?

To add to his confusion, Kenzie suddenly burst out laughing, although it sounded forced. Then she punched her ex's arm. "Greg, that's possibly the worst joke you ever made."

"Ow!" Greg grabbed hold of his arm where she'd hit him and rubbed it. "What? What joke? I didn't make a joke!" When Kenzie gave him an over-the-top version of her angry mom face, Greg took the hint and laughed unconvincingly. "Oh! Um, yeah, that was an incredibly silly thing to say." Jonah got the impression he still had no idea what he'd done.

Pippa gave Greg a playful slap on the leg. "Stop being silly, Daddy!" She grabbed his hand, and with a head-spinning change of subject, she added, "Come see where we live!"

"Oh!" Greg looked at Kenzie, who seemed dazed but nodded assent. "Um, show me the way, I guess."

"Can Frankie come, too?" Dropping Greg's hand, Pippa came over to Jonah and looked up, puzzled. "Why do you look so funny, Mr. Raymond? Are you still mad at me?"

Breathless, Jonah gazed down at the little girl as if he'd never seen her before. She was identical to Kenzie in every way. Except the eyes. Instead of intense blue like her mother's, they were a deep chocolate brown.

Like his.

Was she really his child? Only Kenzie could give him the answer, but he had the very strong sense that Greg's announcement had not been a joke.

"Mr. Raymond?" Pippa tugged at his hand. "Can Frankie please come? My daddy is with us, so he'll make sure we don't run away. And I promise we won't anyway. Please?"

Frankie took his other hand. "Please, Daddy? I promise I'll be good."

Jonah's baffled gaze moved to his son. Did he have a big sister? Even though they weren't related by blood, the two children had grown so close and loved each other as much as if they were siblings.

His throat too clogged with emotion to allow him to speak, Jonah simply nodded. Both children hugged his legs, then dragged a clearly reluctant Greg Halloran into Kenzie's apartment.

Which left him and Kenzie alone in the foyer.

They stood in silence for a moment, both studying the floor near their respective feet. Finally Kenzie let go of the banister and moved to him, chin raised and shoulders squared in the attitude he remembered so well.

"Guess we should talk."

Wordless, Jonah pushed open the door to his apartment and went straight to the kitchen table. After pulling out a chair for Kenzie, he sat next to her and waited. She seemed to be at a rare loss for words.

Finally Jonah broke the silence. He had to ask, even though he was pretty sure of the answer.

"Is it true?"

Shoulders still squared in defiance, Kenzie gave him a single, brief nod.

It was the answer he expected, but Jonah's heart leaped at

her confirmation. "Is that what was in all the messages and letters I never saw?"

She cleared her throat. "At first I just said we needed to talk ASAP. When you didn't answer, I started saying it was urgent, I missed you and wanted to move back to Boston. Which was the truth." After a hard swallow, she went on. "The certified letter said I was pregnant with your child and needed to know if you wanted to be part of her life."

Jonah had stopped breathing as Kenzie spoke. He inhaled deeply as he realized how much damage Elena's protective interference had done. "And you thought I got the letter because it looked like I signed for it."

Kenzie nodded. "I'd told Greg all about it at work one day. I mean, he was my boss, so… I was freaking out, needless to say. He said if I didn't hear from you within the week, he'd marry me."

Jonah felt a dart of jealousy. "Were you seeing him?"

"Well, you know we were dating when I met you, but I thought he was too serious for me, so I broke it off." She blushed. "When I got to San Francisco and found he was a studio head, I realized why I'd gotten such a great job offer. He said he'd never gotten over me and he'd be the best husband and father if I said yes."

"Which you did, when you didn't hear from me." Jonah felt sickened by the thought of another man marrying Kenzie but forced himself to look at it from her perspective. "You did what you needed to do."

Kenzie shook her head. "I could have gone it alone. Lots of women do. But…well, Greg's a good guy and I thought we'd both be better off. So yes, I married him. And it was good for a few years, but after a while he told me he wanted a family of his own." She shrugged. "Then I got sick and lost every baby we conceived, and he got tired of me being sick all the time. So he moved on."

Jonah couldn't keep the bitterness out of his voice. "Nice."

"Honestly, I can't blame him. And he was completely up-front with me when he and Camilla got involved." Kenzie blinked as if warding off tears. "He's been a decent father to Pippa, if a bit lacking in affection." She leaned back in her chair and mumbled to the table, "Of course, she has no idea he's not really her father."

Another emotion jabbed at Jonah's heart. "She's mine," he whispered.

"Yup." A tear trickled down one freckled cheek as Kenzie tried to smile. "That sassy little troublemaker is fifty percent your doing."

Despite the ache in his chest, Jonah chuckled. "Frankie is going to be thrilled."

"But what about you?" Kenzie's anxious tone belied her defiant expression. "Neither of us is exactly your favorite person right now. Do you want her to know? If so, how do we tell her?"

Kenzie was asking all the right questions, but Jonah didn't feel like he had the answers. He was still reeling from Greg's revelation, so much that his head felt as if it were literally spinning. He didn't notice Kenzie had stood up until she leaned over to speak softly in his ear.

"I know it's a big shock," she whispered. "It's important that you take your time. Give it all the thought you need. When you know what you want, let me know."

"No." Jonah sat up straight, realizing the unfairness of his reaction. "No, that's absurd. Pippa is my daughter. She deserves to know the truth."

As he got to his feet, the front door burst open and Frankie came running in, clearly unhappy. "That mean man made my Pippa cry," he informed Kenzie, "and now he's going away."

Chapter Nineteen

Launching into protective mode, Kenzie shot out to the foyer and ran smack into Greg, who was pulling on his coat as he headed to the door.

"What did you say to her?" Kenzie demanded.

"I told her I wouldn't be visiting again." Greg seemed pretty calm for a man who'd just devastated a child.

Kenzie had to restrain herself from grabbing her ex and shaking him. "Why on earth would you tell her that?"

Not even deigning to glance at her, Greg buttoned his overcoat and took his car keys out of his pocket. "Because it's time for her to know the truth, Kenzie. I'm not her father." He nodded toward Jonah's apartment, behind her. "Why should we continue the charade when her real father is right there?"

Kenzie felt the color drain from her face. "Did you tell her that? I thought you'd gotten the message earlier, when I pretended you were joking."

"No, I didn't tell her," Greg said in his most pompous voice. "I'll leave that to the two of you. After all, you've pretty much moved in together, as far as I can tell."

"No, we have not." Jonah's voice made Kenzie jump. She hadn't realized he'd followed her out into the foyer. "And I resent your implying anything like that."

Greg walked over and looked up at Jonah, who seemed to have grown even taller, towering over the spiteful little man.

"And I resent you not taking responsibility for your child. It's about time you did, don't you think?"

"I would have been doing it all along if I'd gotten any of Kenzie's messages," Jonah responded in an even tone. "But trust me, I will from now on. If you're so callous that you can tell a seven-year-old who believes you're her father that you'll never see her again, it's best that you get out of her life and stay out."

Greg stiffened, clearly offended. "My sentiments exactly." Kenzie could see that Greg was trying to stay cool, but that Jonah's characterization had rattled him.

"And I certainly hope you're a better father to your new baby than you were to Pippa today."

Greg's lips disappeared. Without another word, he turned on his heel and strode through the front door. A moment later they heard his car crunch its way out of the drive and turn onto the road.

Kenzie looked up at Jonah. "I'd better go see to Pippa."

Jonah nodded. "Frankie's gone back over there with her. Should I come along?"

She had to think about it for a moment, then gave him a quick nod. "Maybe we should talk to her together, now. Maybe it would make her feel better."

Jonah's big, warm hand on her back comforted Kenzie as they entered her apartment, where Pippa sobbed disconsolately on the oversize sofa as Frankie petted her. The boy gave a worried glance at the grown-ups. "She won't stop crying."

Kenzie sat on Pippa's right, Jonah to the left of Frankie, bookending their children. "Baby girl," Kenzie whispered, "I'm so sorry he said that to you."

Pippa half crawled onto her mother's lap and rubbed at her eyes. "Why's he being so mean to me?" she whimpered. "He doesn't want to see me ever again because he's going to have a new baby."

Kenzie took a deep breath. "Pippa, we have something to tell you that might be hard for you to understand. You can ask all the questions you like, but we might not be able to explain everything very well."

Pippa sat up straight, her tear-streaked face solemn and fearful. "Did you find out you're really, really sick, Mommy?"

"What? No!" Kenzie hugged Pippa, horrified at the question. "I'm going to be fine, I promise. What we have to tell you is something good, but it might take you a while to think so."

The little girl's eyes grew enormous looking from Kenzie to Jonah and back. "Is what my daddy said true? I mean…" She paused as if puzzling over how to phrase the question. "Is Mr. Raymond my real daddy?"

Over the children's heads, Kenzie's eyes met Jonah's. So Pippa had caught on after all. Or maybe Greg had just gone ahead and told her, like the clueless person he was. "Yes, Pips. It's true."

They all watched as Pippa processed the idea. Confusion chased happiness across her thoughtful little face.

"It's okay if you need time to think about it, sweetie," Kenzie murmured. "He only just found out, too."

"But, Pippa." Frankie tugged excitedly at her hand. "That means you're really my big sister!"

Pippa turned her startled brown eyes to Frankie. Joy slowly took over her face and she squealed and threw her arms around her little brother.

Once she'd calmed down, Pippa turned to Kenzie. "So, Mommy, are you going to marry Mr. Raymond?"

Kenzie found herself speechless for a moment, felt her cheeks turning pink. Finally she managed to choke out, "Um… well, no…that's not…" She couldn't look at Jonah.

"But aren't mommies and daddies supposed to be married?"

"Yes!" Frankie seconded. "They definitely have to get married."

Jonah cleared his throat. "Uh… son, remember our talk the other day? It takes time for grown-ups to make big decisions like that."

Frankie's dark eyebrows furrowed. "But—"

Jonah cut him off deftly. "No buts. And no more questions about that, please."

Pippa and Frankie exchanged a puzzled glance. When Pippa's mouth opened, Kenzie gave her the mom look that made her close her mouth immediately.

In a gentle tone, Kenzie said, "Whether we're married or not, he's still your father. And Frankie and Jolie are your little brother and sister."

That made Pippa leap from the sofa and bounce for joy. "Is Jolie still upstairs?" When Jonah nodded, she grabbed Frankie's hand. "Come on! Let's go see our little sister!" She stopped just short of the door and turned back. "What do I call Diane and Paul now?"

Jonah grinned. "Auntie Diane and Uncle Paul. And their baby will be your cousin!"

Pippa's mouth dropped open in amazement. Kenzie's heart warmed at the sight of her little girl's elation. She'd never had any extended family before, since Kenzie was an only child and both her parents had died years ago. Suddenly Pippa's relatives had more than doubled in number. She stood there stunned for a moment. Then she grabbed Frankie's hand and dragged him through the door so she could break the news to her new family.

All three Holiday Farm families held an impromptu celebration for their newly discovered connections. Kenzie was surprised at how eagerly Pippa adjusted to her change of fathers, maybe because Greg hadn't been part of her life for a while already. He'd certainly never been as affectionate as Jonah, who came with a ready-made little brother and sister for Pippa to dote on.

As the children chatted happily with Paul and Diane in the spacious upstairs living room, Jonah subtly maneuvered Kenzie onto one of the settees.

"I'd call this an eventful day," he observed dryly.

Kenzie looked confused for a moment, then suddenly seemed to recall all that had happened. "Ya think?"

"How are you feeling?"

"Overwhelmed, but in a good way." She met his eyes. "They gave me something at the ER that got rid of the headache and body pain. I guess it's still working."

Her defiant look reminded Jonah of his earlier anger. "I might have overreacted."

Kenzie thought it over, shook her head. "No. I understand how scary that must have been for Frankie and you. But honestly, I never touched one of those pain pills. I thought about it a few times when the pain was horrible, but I always decided against it."

"Then why did you have them right next to your bed?" He couldn't keep the worry out of his voice.

"Because the pain kept getting worse. But the reason I didn't take them was that I know how sensitive I am to medication." Kenzie sighed, looking regretful. "Which is why taking a second pill last night made it extremely hard for me to wake up."

"Ah." Relief lightened Jonah's heart at her explanation.

"When I got home, I gave the vial of painkillers to Paul so he can dispose of them safely."

His heart lightened more. "I'm sorry I flew off the handle."

"I get it." Kenzie gave him a rueful smile. "I remember flying off the handle myself about eight years ago."

"Oh, that?" Jonah grimaced. "I have been wondering. I mean, I was planning to propose after your graduation ceremony. I was stunned when you blew up at me."

Now Kenzie was staring at him in surprise. "You were going to propose?"

Feigning nonchalance, he lifted his shoulder. "That was my plan."

Kenzie flopped back on the settee, covering her face with her hands. "Unbelievable."

"What?"

"The reason I got myself so worked up and mad that I took that job and moved away is that you didn't propose after our camping trip." She removed her hands to reveal a blush staining her cheeks. "When you didn't—even after I told you about the job—I'm afraid I made a very foolish decision."

"So that's why you were so mad at me?" He chuckled. "And I had gone home specifically to get my grandmother's engagement ring. It was in my pocket when you dumped me."

"What?" Kenzie's expression was a mixture of surprise and regret. "Now I feel even worse!"

Jonah considered her words and remembered his own pointless regrets about Elena. "What happened, happened. Focusing on the past doesn't accomplish anything." He reached for her hand. "But I hope you're still feeling better. I guess last night was pretty bad."

She winced at the memory. "It was the worst."

"I can't believe you felt that ill and didn't ask for my help." Distraught, Jonah squeezed her hand. "I guess you don't trust me enough to do that."

She laced her fingers through his. "It's not that. I'm just so used to being independent, I hate to ask for help. I don't want anyone to know what a mess I am." Glancing down at their entwined hands, she whispered, "Especially you."

"I guess we both have a few things to sort out," Jonah murmured. "I'd love it if we can sort them out together."

Kenzie looked up at him, her eyes bright with hopeful tears.

"I would love that, too, but I need some time to process everything."

Jonah sighed. "You're right, of course. I say let's have no regrets and look ahead instead of back."

A smile lit up her face. "Speaking of looking ahead, the harvest pageant is coming up and we still have a lot to do!"

Chapter Twenty

A few days before the harvest pageant, Kenzie learned she had been right all along. According to the tests and scans Paul had ordered, she had had Lyme disease for quite a while, long enough for the bacteria to wreak havoc.

By the time she got the results, she'd already been on antibiotics for almost a week, again thanks to Paul. It would take a while to see any significant improvement, but now that she knew what was wrong with her, Jonah noticed that she seemed much more optimistic and less stressed. She told him she was relieved to know what had been causing all those weird symptoms, but she admitted that she was even more relieved to know they weren't psychosomatic.

Since Kenzie was still feeling wobbly, she had leaned more and more on Jonah to get the harvest pageant on its feet. Jonah found himself grateful for the distraction. It forced him to focus on accomplishing tasks rather than thinking about the future. Working so closely with Kenzie and Pippa in the weeks before the pageant gave him time to observe and interact with them both. And he had to admit he liked what he saw. A lot.

The more he got to know Pippa, the prouder he was to be her father. When he'd apologized to her for his anger, she'd graciously accepted his apology and opened her heart to him as her real daddy.

They'd asked the kids to keep quiet about Mr. Raymond

being Pippa's father, knowing it might raise questions they weren't prepared to answer. But even though they weren't officially siblings, Frankie and Pippa's bond kept growing stronger. Jonah was amazed how much his troubled boy blossomed in a short time. Habitual moodiness was replaced with frequent laughter and a silly streak Jonah had never seen before. It was clear Frankie already saw Kenzie as his mother and ran to her for cuddles and comfort almost as often as he ran to Jonah.

Jolie was still Jolie, and Jonah loved to see Kenzie scoop her up and cover her with kisses as if she were Kenzie's own baby. The hungry, lost look no longer appeared on her face when she held Jolie in her arms. Instead, she looked deeply content.

On a gorgeous Sunday afternoon in late October, the Good Shepherd students clustered in the church vestibule to enter for the harvest pageant. All dressed up in their costumes and masks, they were more than ready to perform. The fourth and fifth graders looked adorable as the farmers and their families. The second and third graders wore angel costumes, and the first graders wore farm animal masks they'd created themselves.

Kenzie and Jonah beamed at the excited group. "Everyone take hands," Kenzie stage-whispered, knowing the pews were packed with excited parents and parishioners. The kids squirmed around to find hands to hold until they formed a ragged circle. "I'm going to say a quick prayer and I want you all to listen and pray along with me silently. Okay?"

When they all nodded, Kenzie cleared her throat and squeezed Jonah's hand.

"Dear Lord, please bless us as we perform our little pageant. Help us to keep You first in our hearts and give thanks for all Your blessings. Amen."

Most of the children mumbled "amen" after Kenzie finished, but one little voice shouted it out.

"A-men!"

When the other children giggled, Pippa shrugged her angel wings. "God made me loud," she said philosophically, "so I guess He wants me to shout."

"Okay, is everyone ready?" Farmer hats, tinsel halos and animal ears nodded. "Let's go! Farmers first."

The farmers walked solemnly up the aisle to the altar and recited their lines with innocent conviction. Then the white-robed angels filed in singing simple hymns of praise and encouraging the farmers.

Kenzie felt tears spring to her eyes as she listened to the childish voices singing. Her own little girl sang a bit more lustily than the others as she held the hands of the angels on either side of her. Kenzie felt Jonah's arm slip around her shoulders as he whispered, "That's our girl."

Finally the animals danced their way to the altar, evoking laughter and applause from the audience. Even shy Frankie sang out happily from behind his horse mask and gave a spontaneous whinny when he reached the altar.

As the lights came back on, Kenzie could hear happy chatter coming from the pews. Jonah put his arms around her and kissed the top of her head.

"I think God answered your prayer."

His arms stayed around her when she turned to look up at him. "I couldn't have done it without you."

Jonah's eyes crinkled as he smiled down at her. "Wow, whatever happened to Miss Independence?"

Feeling suddenly shy, Kenzie returned his smile. "I guess the teacher learned a few lessons herself."

He nodded, his face softening. "This one did as well."

For a moment they gazed into each other's eyes. Then Jonah bent down and she stood on her toes to meet his kiss halfway. While holding each other close Kenzie felt a deep, solid peace fill her heart and soul.

Her reverie was interrupted by someone tapping on her shoulder. She turned to see Enid staring at her, a look of displeasure stamped on her features. "Everyone wants you two to come take a bow, which you very much deserve. Then I think we need to have another talk."

Jonah grabbed Kenzie's hand and led her up the aisle to the altar, where the children burst into applause, then ran over to engulf their teachers with hugs. Parents and fellow teachers came up to the altar and mingled with them, thanking and congratulating everyone for their hard work. Many asked when the next pageant would be.

The school's first ever public performance was a big success.

Gradually the children and audience filtered out. Diane and Paul, who had watched the show with little Jolie, took Pippa and Frankie back to the farm, leaving Kenzie and Jonah alone with Enid Mullin.

"Let's sit down," the headmistress suggested, indicating the way to the front row of pews. She pulled the piano bench out so she could face the two teachers, her arms crossed. "I think you need to tell me what's going on here. Do you remember the talks we had not long ago, where each of you insisted that there was no way you'd get together again?"

Fighting down memories of being in trouble with her high school principal, Kenzie raised her head. "Jonah is Pippa's father."

Enid's large eyes grew even larger. She opened her mouth but no words came out.

"Jonah and Pippa only found out a little over a week ago." Kenzie's cheeks were burning, but she kept her gaze fixed on the headmistress. "And Frankie knows, but he and Pippa know not to tell the other kids for now."

"I see." Enid's voice was nearly a whisper. She unfolded her arms and coughed, her eyes switching back and forth between Kenzie and Jonah. "Well. Needless to say, I wasn't prepared for this, um, explanation." Her forehead furrowed and she tapped her foot, studying the burgundy carpet as she thought. Finally she looked up. "You're right to keep this quiet. I'm still getting over the shock of finding you two in an obviously nonplatonic embrace, but with this new information..." Enid sighed, shaking her head. "I can understand that there's a bond, and I hope it leads to happiness for both of you." She leaned toward Jonah and Kenzie, a humorous sparkle in her dark eyes. "And if there's a wedding, I hope you'll let my husband do the honors."

Epilogue

In the weeks that followed, Kenzie's health continued to improve in fits and starts. The good spells lasted longer and the bad spells became rarer as time passed. She was able to throw herself into preparation for the Christmas pageant, once again with Jonah's help.

This time the classes were divided into the people at the manger—the holy family, shepherds and wise men—angels and friendly beasts. They learned Christmas carols from other countries as well as the more popular ones for the audience sing-along.

The more time she and Jonah spent together, the more Kenzie found herself loving and trusting him. His generous heart and tenderness toward the children and herself felt like the best gift of all. Now that they'd forgiven each other for past misunderstandings, there was no longer a barrier between them. Kenzie had no doubt they would be together for a long time, and the knowledge made her wait patiently for the day it became official.

One Sunday a few days before Christmas, the Good Shepherd Church was packed not only with parents and teachers, but with people from the whole Chapelton community. After hearing everyone rave about the harvest pageant, they were eager to see the children's Christmas performance.

The audience's energy encouraged the children to put everything they had into the pageant. They recited their lines and sang their songs with unrestrained joy, and everyone rose and sang along with the more familiar carols.

The headmistress wiped more than one tear from her eyes as the pageant ended. She came over to the vestry where Jonah and Kenzie stood and gave them her biggest beaming smile. "You two go up there and take a bow. You deserve it." And Kenzie was pretty sure Enid winked at Jonah as she sent them down the aisle.

Holding hands, they bowed along with the children. Then to Kenzie's astonishment, Jonah got down on one knee and pulled a little velvet box from his pocket. The children around them and the audience in the pews gasped.

"I know what it is!" Frankie shouted as he ran to his father's side. "C'mon, Pippa!"

"Oh!" Pippa exclaimed, rushing to stand by her mother. "Mommy, you hafta say yes, okay? Please?"

The onlookers chuckled, then fell silent, seeming to hold their breath.

"Mackenzie Reid," Jonah said. "I should have asked you this eight years ago. I hope it's not too late."

Kenzie's eyes sparkled and her smile grew almost too big for her face. "It isn't."

Opening the box, Jonah held it up to her. "I'd like my family to marry your family. Will you marry us, Kenzie and Pippa?"

"Yes!" Pippa yelled at the top of her lungs.

Everyone burst out laughing, then stopped as Kenzie gazed lovingly at Jonah. "We will."

The sanctuary exploded with applause as Jonah rose to his feet, slipped the antique ring on Kenzie's finger and threw his arms around her.

"Are you happy?" Jonah whispered into Kenzie's ear.

"Are you kidding?" Kenzie pulled back to show him her glowing face. "I have the love of my life back, my little girl has her daddy, and we have the love of a beautiful family. I've never felt so happy in my entire life."

"Thank God," Jonah murmured, kissing her cheek.

"I do," Kenzie whispered. "With all my heart."

* * * * *

Dear Reader,

Sometimes we look back and wonder what might have happened if we'd dealt with a difficult situation differently. Kenzie reacted with anger, Jonah with hurt acceptance. What if they'd been honest instead of lashing out?

On the other hand, would Jonah and Kenzie have found faith if they'd been together all along? Adversity doesn't always lead to God, but it can if we seek Him and find solace in His presence.

Christ teaches us forgiveness, honesty, kindness and patience. We live in a time of hair-trigger reactions where it's rare to see these virtues. I loved writing these characters because when they opened their hearts to God, they confronted their faults and worked to overcome them.

I hope you enjoyed the journey of these two fractured families finding healing together. Thank you for reading my book, and God bless you.

Lillian Warner